Rembert

The Book and the Play

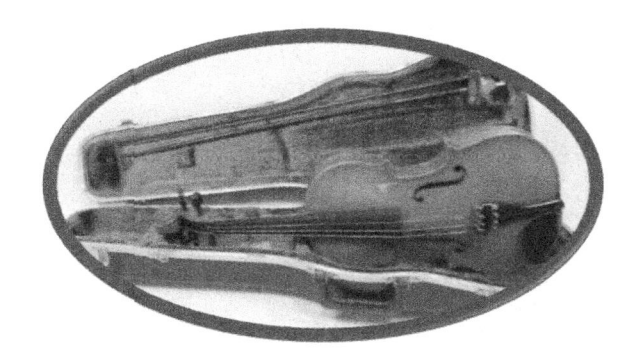

A True Mystery Story About Rembert, the "Stradivarius Wurlitzer" and a Red Stradivarius Violin with a Play Explaining All

The man who came from a family making musical instruments for over 400 years,
The man who sold more authenticated Stradivari violins than anyone else ever,
The man who doubtless discovered the famous *Mendelssohn* violin of legend,
The man who for decades was the world's authority on Stradivari violins,
The man who for decades was the authority on Stradivari instruments,
This man may have traded a quarter of all known Strad violins.
This man is a principal in a mystery story about a red violin;
This man was "The Resurrector of *The Mendelssohn*."

By Frederick Pabst Wurlitzer, M.D., F.A.C.S.

Publishing History

Edition 4 / March 2021
ISBN: 9798598087749

All Rights Reserved.

Copyright @ 2021 Frederick Pabst Wurlitzer

No part of this book may be reproduced or transmitted in any form or by any means, electronic or mechanical, including photocopying, recording or any information storage and retrieval system, without permission in writing from the author.

Dedication

This book and play are dedicated to Rembert Wurlitzer and his widow Lee. Both have now passed away.

Acknowledgements

I would like to acknowledge the grandson of Rudolph Henry Wurlitzer, William Griess, who contributed a significant number of details about Wurlitzer family history, and Marianne Wurlitzer, the daughter of Rembert Wurlitzer, who added more details. Mr. David Fulton provided details of the provenance of *The Mendelssohn* and the history of *La Pucelle*, a Stradivari he had owned. Finally, I acknowledge Terry Hathaway who helped materially with early editing of the book, and Bill Smart who enabled publishing brilliantly.

Books by Fred Pabst Wurlitzer

Philosophical Poetry
The Gospel of Fred – 2019
The Second Gospel of Fred - 2019
Love to the Trinity – 2020
Non-Fiction
Rembert – 2020
(Includes the play, *Rembert*)
Children's Books
Spiritual Fairy Tales – 2020
The Seven Deadly Sins – 2020
The Seven Heavenly Virtues – 2020
Stories from the Old Testament
Comic Books with Doggerel
Book 1 Genesis - Part 1 – 2020
Book 2 Genesis - Part 2 – 2020
Book 3 Exodus - Part 2 – 2020
Book 4 Exodus - Part 2 – 2020
Book 5 Number and Deuteronomy– 2020
Book 6 Joshua – 2020
Book 7 Ruth – 2020
Albrecht Dürer's "Kleine Passion" – 2020
Albrecht Dürer's "Grosse Passion" – 2020
Han Holbein's "Dance of Death" – 2020
Albrecht Dürer's "The Crucifixion" – 2020

Table of Contents

Foreword vii
A Review from Mr. David Fulton viii

Chapter 1 – Brief Wurlitzer Family History 1
Chapter 2 – Rembert's Background 7
Chapter 3 – Two Suspects in the Red Violin Mystery 13
Chapter 4 – Rembert's Discovery of a Stradivari Violin 19
Chapter 5 – Another Mystery: Why was the Red Violin
  not Entered into the Wurlitzer and
  Rembert's Inventory? 21
Chapter 6 – Pros and Cons Regarding the Argument that
  Rembert Found a Red Stradivarius Violin
  around 1926 that Turned Out to Be
  The Mendelssohn. 25
Chapter 7 – The Very Entertaining
  Francesco Mendelssohn. 31

Rembert 35
   Introduction 37
   To the Play 37
   Plot and Scenes 41
   Family Tree 41
   Opening 44

   SCENE #1 47
   SCENE #2 55
   SCENE #3 65
   SCENE #4 73

SCENE #5	83
SCENE #6	90
SCENE #7	97
Intermezzo	117
Chapter 8 – Are Strads Good Investments?	119
Chapter 9 – How Many Strads Were Made?	121
Chapter 10 – Authentications and Forgeries	123
Chapter 11 – How Many Stradivari Violins Did a Wurlitzer Find, Authenticate, Buy, or Sell on Consignment?	129
Chapter 12 – Fulton Coments	133
Chapter 13 – Resources	135
Chapter 14 – Provenance of the Red Violin	139
Appendix 1 – Tarisio Records	141
Appendix 2 – Fulton Provenance Presented by Mr. David Fulton.	147
Appendix 3 – Combined Provenance from All Sources of *The Mendelssohn*	155
Appendix 4 – An Incomplete List of 135 Stradivari Violins Owned or Sold by a Wurlitzer According to Goodkind and Tarisio	161
Appendix 5 – Bibliography	173
Addendum 1 – Epilogue	177
About the Author	179

Foreword

While I was growing up, my father told me a number of stories about his first cousin Rembert, who was my first cousin once removed. Some of these stories related to the Wurlitzer Music Company, but one of the most memorable stories was about Rembert finding a red violin.

The play beginning after Chapter 7 of this book presents what I think really happened around the time of Rembert's discovery of the real *Red Violin*. This play is in part a biography of an extraordinary man based on facts expanded upon by speculation. It is the first play I have ever written.

Some readers may have found the play confusing without having read a portion of the book. So, Chapters 1-7 provide first a brief history of the Wurlitzer Family and Rembert, and arguments supporting my belief that the red violin my father witnessed Rembert discovering was *The Mendelssohn.*

Later chapters address concerns and questions some readers may have. Finally, in Appendix 3, I give my rendering of an updated provenance for *The Mendelssohn.*

In part, this book is a detective story attempting to identify the real red violin that became the basis for the movie *The Red Violin* and my play Rembert. The book gives a few interesting details about Wurlitzer family history.

Mostly, this book and play are about a man who became totally infatuated and obsessed with rare violins.

A Review from Mr. David Fulton

The World's Greatest Current Collector of Rare Musical Instruments
and
World Renown Rare Violin Expert

August 28, 2020

Fred,

Congratulations!

I have read your magnum opus now and can find nothing to add. A magnum opus it is. It is certainly the most detailed discussion of the provenance and history of a single violin I've ever read. And, of course, the 1720 Mendelssohn could indeed been the inspiration for "The Red Violin" mythos. I think the your "Rembert" play will be interesting to many people. Fascinating stuff. It will be fun to see what's entailed in getting it produced and even more fun to see it on stage. Perhaps sometime after this miserable COVID-19 business has passed

I do agree that your editor's opinion that the play should come first is absolutely correct. Your labyrinthine investigation into the wild, wild west of fiddle lore, fascinating to you and to me, may be a bit much for normal folk (i.e. non-violin-aficionados) to digest. Probably the essay is best read after the play has presented Rembert's story so completely and well. Putting the essay first would be like having them read Tolkien's lengthy appendices before reading the "Lord of the Rings."

Again, my heartiest congratulations. "Rembert" is an amazing display of intellectual insight, vigor and energy for a man of your age, indeed of any age. It is very good work indeed. Remarkable.

I hope it really does transpire that we have lunch one fine post-COVID day.

Dave

Chapter 1

Brief Wurlitzer Family History

Allow me to begin many years ago by relating some of my family's connections with music.

Farny Wurlitzer (1883–1972), my great uncle and CEO of The Wurlitzer Company years after my grandfather, Howard Wurlitzer (1871–1928) died, traced with the help of my great uncle Rudolph Henry Wurlitzer (1873–1948), a family tree back to the ancient Teutonic knights' family of Wurr of Nürnberg or Nuremberg, around 1000 C.E. My personal DNA analysis suggests a Viking ancestry.

"*Itz*," in old German, may have meant "a place," like "*plātz*" and "*er*" probably meant "from," so the "*Wurlitzers*" were from places where the family named "Wurr" had lived.

The old Wurr knights and early Wurlitzers had a beautifully distinctive coat of arms. On the back of this painting below of the family coat of arms that Farny gave me years ago, he wrote the family tree. Wurlitzers first started making musical instruments about 400 years ago.

A painting commissioned by Farny Wurlitzer

The first Wurlitzer, after the Wurr's, was Heinrich Wurlitzer born in 1596, and then Nicolaus Wurlitzer, born in 1659, who made musical instruments. Heinrich probably made musical instruments before Nicolaus, although that is not recorded.

In John H. Fairfield's, *Known Violin Makers*, published in New York in 1942, and adding to the Wurlitzer family tree, Mr. Fairfield states that John George Wurlitzer, who was born in 1726, followed the craft of violin making. Hans Adam Wurlitzer was elected in 1701 to membership in the lute makers' guild of Saxony, and in 1732 he was identified as a master violin maker.[1] There were other Wurlitzer music makers besides Nicolaus, John, and Hans. Another member of the family, Frederick Wurlitzer, my namesake, was a child musical prodigy who toured Europe in concert presentations and became the court pianist to Frederick the Great of Prussia at the age of sixteen.

From father to oldest son following primogeniture, and sometimes younger sons, Wurlitzer music craftsmanship, musical instrument sales, and performing took place over four centuries. Making musical instruments was a home business. In East Germany, the name "Wurlitzer" became a word synonymous with a musical instrument maker, or someone involved somehow with music.

In 1856, after emigrating from Schöneck in 1853, Franz Rudolph founded the Rudolph Wurlitzer Company that is usually referred to as

---

[1] Presto-Times, Page 9, May-June 1933.

simply "Wurlitzer" or the "Wurlitzer Music Company" that came to be listed on the NYSE.[2] [3]

About 30 years ago when I visited Schöneck ("beautiful corner") in East Germany, the home of Franz Rudolph Wurlitzer, founder of the Wurlitzer Company, I saw musical instruments over 200 years old with the name of Wurlitzer on them in the nearby museum, the Musikinstrumenten-Museum Markneukirchen in Saxony. The story of Wurlitzers making musical instruments including violins as "*Geigenbaumeisters*" (i.e., expert violin makers) starting about 400 years ago is a remarkable one. Although I was trained as a surgical oncologist, I remain intrigued by Wurlitzer history.

When I was a boy, my father, Raimund Wurlitzer (1896 – 1986) who was the only son of Franz Rudolph Wurlitzer's eldest son Howard Wurlitzer, told me many stories about the Wurlitzer Music Company and, in particular, stories about Rembert Wurlitzer (1904 – 1963), who discovered a red Stradivarius violin. In this book I attempt to prove that the red violin Rembert identified was the famous *Mendelssohn*.

One time, my father told me that at a Wurlitzer Board meeting, a discussion arose about what to name Wurlitzer player-piano rolls. My grandfather, Howard, the CEO, suggested "ABC" rolls. My father suggested a more original name, "QRS," and so Wurlitzer piano rolls became "QRS rolls" at my father's suggestion. This may not seem like a very big deal, but it is for many theater organ society members.

Other stories followed, but this is not the place to recount them. It astounds me that among American Theatre Organ Society members

---

[2] https://en.wikipedia.org/wiki/Wurlitzer.
[3] Although Wikipedia states Rudolph Wurlitzer founded his company in 1853, that date is incorrect. Rudolph arrived on the Adolphine from Bremen in June 1853. After working for other people for about three years, he actually started his company the Rudolph Wurlitzer Company in 1856.

and other organ society members worldwide, there is such fascination with Wurlitzer family history.

Wurlitzer became a leading international center for rare string instruments under Rudolph Henry, Rembert's father. It bought, held on consignment, sold, authenticated, and/or restored more than half the world's 600 known Stradivari (not all violins), and supplied instruments to Fritz Kreisler, David Oistrakh, and Isaac Stern, among others[4]. Wurlitzer's rare violin acquisitions were independently directed by Rembert after 1926.

Rudolph Wurlitzer Company's 1929 purchase of the famous Wanamaker Collection of forty-four stringed instruments that was at the time the finest collection of Stradivari, Amati, and other old violins in the world put Wurlitzer in the forefront of major rare instrument purchases and sales.

My father's childhood languages were first German and secondly English. Rembert became fluent in German later. The two of them sometimes went to Germany in the 1920s for business, pleasure, or to visit family. There was the "Clarinet Wurlitzer," and in East Germany, many Wurlitzer relatives. Rudolph Henry had gone to violin school in Berlin, and Rembert followed with studies in Europe in the 1920s.

After East Germany opened up following reunification in 1990, I met Wurlitzers who had survived World War II. In Vienna, there were other Wurlitzers who lived on Wurlitzergasse (i.e., Wurlitzer Alley or Lane).[5] German connections were ongoing among American Wurlitzers, who often communicated with their German kin. My mother, whose first language was also German, did so routinely.

In 1960, Farny started in Hüllhorst a German branch of the Wurlitzer Company called "Deutsche Wurlitzer." That division

---

[4] https://en.wikipedia.org/wiki/Rembert_Wurlitzer_Co.
[5] https://www.geschichtewiki.wien.gv.at/Wurlitzergasse.

became a reason for Farny, who became President in 1932, to go to Germany often until his death in 1972. The Gibson Guitar Corporation controls the Wurlitzer brand now.

Wurlitzer went on to make jukeboxes, mighty Wurlitzer organs and a multitude of other musical interests. It is not the purpose of this book to expand upon Wurlitzer instrument production. It is time to turn to Rembert.

Chapter 2

Rembert's Background

Rembert was born in Cincinnati as the only son of Rudolph Henry Wurlitzer (1873–1948), who, in turn, was the second son of Franz Rudolph Wurlitzer (1831–1914) founder of the Wurlitzer Music Company.

Rembert dropped out of Princeton so he could become more of an authority on rare violins. After studying violins and violin-making in Mirecourt, France, in Italy and Germany, and then in England for two and a half years,[6] studying under the then-leading violin expert of the world, Alfred Hill and later his dad, Rudolph Henry. Rembert also learned shop skills from many violin dealers he visited.

Sometime in the early 1920's, very likely in 1926, Rembert met my father Raimund in Berlin at an outdoor café. It was there that they heard a street musician playing a red violin that Rembert felt was a Stradivarius. This was an impressive find.

Alfred Hill was so impressed with the young Rembert's knowledge about rare violins and industriousness that he asked him to join W.E. Hill & Sons, but Rembert respectfully declined. He chose instead to accept a job offer from Wurlitzer in 1926 as head of acquisitions, allegedly over his father Rudolph.

---

[6] Cited by William Griess, grandson of Rudolph Henry Wurlitzer

These job offers from Hill and Wurlitzer probably followed their recognition that Rembert had discovered a red Stradivarius violin. This otherwise odd corporate structure where Rembert was ahead of his father in acquisitions continued while Rembert learned a great deal more from his dad, Rudolph Henry, at the "Wurlitzer violin finishing school."

I believe that a reasonable explanation for Wurlitzer creating this odd corporate structure was to reward Rembert for not accepting a job offer from Alfred Hill and in recognition of his remarkable find of a red Stradivarius violin. What red Stradivarius Rembert found will be argued in this book.

Rudolph Henry is shown in the Wurlitzer Old Violin Room in 1906.
Rembert learned a great amount from his dad.

For twenty-three years (1926 - 1949), Rembert bought, authenticated and sold, often on consignment, Stradivari instruments aggressively working with Wurlitzer.

Unfortunately, mistakes had become not unheard of at Wurlitzer, but only rarely with Rembert who corrected mistakes by others. One reason why Rembert separated from Wurlitzer was a significant problem from outstanding guarantees on discredited instruments from one employee in particular who had been head of the rare instrument department, curator of the Wurlitzer collection and in charge of repairs, but not authentications. In forming the Rembert Wurlitzer Company in 1949, Rembert was quoted as saying he "didn't want to spend the rest of his life buying back, Jay C. Freeman's mistakes." [7]

Rembert had not hired Mr. Freeman who had become by the mid 1930s "a dilemma" impairing the reputation of Wurlitzer.[8] Rembert was outraged, probably feeling his own reputation was also being demeaned.

In 1949, he formed the Rembert Wurlitzer Company.[9] Over time, Rembert developed an obsessive and possessive interest in Stradivari violins, increasing his unusually insightful knowledge through his ever-growing rare violin purchasing experiences.

After founding the Rembert Wurlitzer Company and buying out the Wurlitzer rare violin department in 1949, Rembert handled other rare musical instruments than Stradivaris, including Guadagninis, Amatis, del Gesùs, Gaglianos, Roccas, Bergonzis, Stainers, Lorenzinis, Guarneris, and Giuseppes.

On September 20, 1953, Rembert temporarily loaned four Stradivari instruments to the La Salle String Quartet so their musicians could play them at a Cincinnati College of Music performance supported by my grandmother, Helene Wurlitzer. According to William Griess, a grandson of Rudolph Henry Wurlitzer (1873 –

---

[7] *Stradivari's Genius* by Toby Faber. Random House Paperback, New York. 2004. Page 194.
[8] https://www.gettyimages.ca/detail/news-photo/photo-shows-a-dilema-for-a-violin-expert-jay-c-freeman-news-photo/540340080.
[9] *Wurlitzer Family History* by Lloyd Graham 1955 in the "Second-Generation" chapter and *New York Herald Tribune* Obituary October 22, 1953.

1948), "These were the *Baron Knoop* violin of 1715, the *Medici* viola of 1690, the *La Pucelle* violin of 1709 and the *Davidoff* cello of 1712." William Griess, whose parents kept the program for this performance, represented to me that these four instruments were used.

That event later confirmed by Mr. Fulton, a previous owner, that Rembert had on consignment, at one time *La Pucelle,* or *"The Virgin."* Mr. David L. Fulton of Seattle has probably the largest collection today of rare musical instruments.[10] The Tarisio Auction house, in its index of rare violins, does not cite Rembert as a past owner or a consignee of *The Virgin*. Nor does Goodkind. Those absences are mistakes, in my opinion, and are representative of the frequent difficulty interpreting inventory lists and records.

Mr. Fulton confirms Rembert had on consignment the other quartet instruments loaned to La Salle. Rembert was a man of great integrity, and even if instruments were on consignment, he would not have exposed them to unnecessary misadventure.

The vast majority of rare musical instruments that Rembert handled were on consignment. Therefore, much ado has been made that Rembert was not a collector or a buyer, but he certainly bought rare musical instruments from time to time. Among the violins the Rembert Wurlitzer Co. owned and then sold was the Henry Hottinger Collection bought in 1967. About thirty violins in all (not all were Stradivari) from that collection were subsequently dispersed all over the world. There is also indisputable evidence that after his death in 1949, there was an extensive inventory, not entirely on consignment, including the *Hellier* Stradivarius that his widow Lee held.[11] Moreover, during his career at Wurlitzer from 1926 to 1949, he purchased on behalf of Wurlitzer an impressive collection of rare

---

[10] https://en.wikipedia.org/wiki/David_L._Fulton.
[11] https://www.nytimes.com/1974/08/13/archives/wurlitzer-to-shut-down-oldinstrument-concern.html

musical instruments. Clearly, although Rembert handled many if not most musical instruments on consignment, he also made purchases.

Chapter 3

Two Suspects in the Red Violin Mystery

Who Owned the Red Violin and When?

Rembert was sitting at an outside café in Berlin with my father around 1926 when a gentleman whom Rembert presumed to be a gypsy started playing a violin – a red violin. Rembert perked up, and then after listening intently, he said to his companions and my father, "That violin may be a Stradivarius." His examination of the violin confirmed it was a Stradivarius.

My main suspect for the red Stradivarius violin that Rembert identified on that occasion is the famous *Mendelssohn.*

The Mendelssohn provenance became convoluted over time. I find it fascinating. Bear with me please as I present plodding detail.

Walter Hamma (1916–1988), a German violin maker and dealer was the first owner of *The Mendelssohn* after *The Mendelssohn*s, according to Tarisio record (#40316). The Fulton Provenance Appendix 2 cites other owners up to 1913 when Francesco Mendelssohn came to own the fiddle. The Fulton Provenance offers no provenances between 1913 and 1990 when Elizabeth Pitcairn became owner.

Mr. Hamma surely visited Berlin from time to time, I suspect it was not often, because his business was in Stuttgart. It was not

Hamma who discovered the red violin in Berlin, I claim, although Tarisio lists him as the first recorded owner of *The Mendelssohn* (Tarisio #40316) and Rembert as the second recorded owner after Lilli and Franz von Mendelssohn.[12] The Tarisio records and Fulton Provenance *for The Mendelssohn* are obviously incomplete. The play at the end of this book expands through reasonable speculations upon the provenance.

It was certainly a coincidence that Rembert, one of the world's greatest authorities on Stradivari instruments, happened to be present when someone played an unknown Stradivari. It was well known that Rembert had a very good ear.

Who actually discovered *The (Red) Mendelssohn*, I did not definitively know initially, except in my opinion, it was not Walter Hamma, but rather Rembert. If I had known initially which red violin for sure, I might cheekily have called it the *"Rembert Red Stradivarius,"* if it was not *The Mendelssohn*, because Rembert discovered a red Stradivarius according to my father. There are few Stradivari violins as red as *The Mendelssohn*. By a process of elimination and other evidence that will be presented, the red Stradivarius Rembert discovered was likely *The Mendelssohn*.

Another suspect that may have no color as *The Mendelssohn* is a Stradivari violin Tarisio #51374, I called initially the *"Unnamed,"* whose provenance began with Rembert. Actually, Tarisio violin #51374 may be *The Comte de Villares of 1720* because the backs as portrayed by Goodkind are similar. Tarisio does not list any earlier owners than Rembert, so who owned this violin before Rembert? It seemed a coincidence that *The Unnamed* and *The Mendelssohn* were both made in 1720. If this unnamed violin is the one Rembert discovered in Berlin at an outdoor cafe, I would rename it also the

---

[12] https://tarisio.com/cozio-archive/property/?ID=40316.

"*Rembert Red Stradivarius*" in order to be consistent in giving Rembert credit.

My prime suspect remained for a considerable period, however, *The Mendelssohn*. It would be interesting indeed, I surmised, if both Tarisio #51374 and #40316 could be shown to be the same violin, Perhaps the two violins were the same, but the backs were not the same. Otherwise, the records of both violins could be combined.

Others have also speculated that the red violin discovered by Rembert was undeniably the "*Red Mendelssohn of 1720*" or just "*The Mendelssohn*" that inspired the movie, *The Red Violin*. Rembert did purchase *The Mendelssohn* in 1956 according to Tarisio, well after selling it, I suspect, to Hamma in Stuttgart in the mid- to late-1920s. My best guess is that the year was 1926 immediately before Rembert was appointed head of Wurlitzer acquisitions.

There is a tendency among dealers to strongly discredit Tarisio records. Although there are certainly many inconsistencies in Tarisio records, there are also many truths. So, when Tarisio lists violins #40316 and #51374 Stradivari of 1720 as being owned by Rembert, or at least consigned to Rembert, I found the Tarisio assertions interesting and more than consistent with a possibility that both suspects being Stradivari of 1720 were the same violin, that is, *The Mendelssohn*. All I had to do to prove the two Tarisio violins are the same violin, I dreamed one night to compare the backs. Unfortunately, the backs were not the same.

The Fulton provenance has no information from 1913 when Francesco Mendelssohn owned *The Mendelssohn* to 1990 when Elizabeth Pitcairn came to own the fiddle. That is an enormous gap in ownership.

Tarisio records for *The Mendelssohn* (Tarisio #40316) clearly show Rembert had bought *The Mendelssohn* from Herr Hamma in 1956. Tarisio records for the unnamed red Stradivarius

#51374 suggests Rembert had been the first owner. Perhaps, then, the violin Rembert found was Tarisio #51274, except that violin is not red in color apparently. It was possible also that my father had been mistaken in saying the violin he witnessed Rembert discovering was a red violin.

But how could I explain the mystery of how Marianne Wurlitzer, daughter of Rembert, could not recall *The Mendelssohn* being in inventory?

Goodkind[13] shows a Wurlitzer was involved with four Stradivari: *The Bishop, The Bavarian, The Madrileno,* and *The Woolhouse.* None of these violins have the same back patterns as shown in the Goodkind book. None of them have a back pattern similar to that of *The Mendelssohn,* as shown by Tarisio.

Tarisio gives the dimensions for *The Mendelssohn*, but not for *The Unnamed,* so, I was unable to compare dimensions. Nonetheless, the patterns of stripes are different. That suggested the prime suspect remained the red violin, *The Mendelssohn.*

---

[13] Goodkind, H.K. *Violin Iconography of Antonio Stradivari.* Page 734

The Two Suspect's Tarisio Provenances

The Mendelssohn

The Tarisio provenance for *The Mendelssohn* Stradivarius, Tarisio violin #40316 affirms that Rembert through his company purchased that red violin in 1956. According to this provenance, Rembert held that red violin until 1990. This Tarisio evidence may confirm that Rembert owned or controled *The Mendelssohn* until his death in 1963, and his wife Lee thereafter to 1973. It is surprising that so much documentation of recent events is missing or just unavailable.

Provenance

-	Lilli von Mendelssohn
-	Franz von Mendelssohn
until 1956	Hamma & Co.
from 1956	Rembert Wurlitzer Inc.
until 1990	Luthier Rosenthal & Son
from 1990	Current owner

From a screenshot of Tarisio site
The Mendelssohn, Tarisio violin #40316

Seven years from 1956 to 1963 is an astonishingly long period of time for a dealer who did not collect rare violins to hold one in his inventory, and then his wife, Lee, held the violin allegedly until her death. This prolonged period of ownership suggests *The Mendelssohn* held special value to Rembert and his wife Lee. The reason, I suggest, is that this was the Stradivari violin Rembert identified as a youth.

The Unnamed

Tarisio #51374 remains a mystery. The earliest owner according to Tarisio was Rembert. Was this the Stradivari violin Rembert found? I might say so, except photos suggest it is not red. Perhaps, my father's or my recollection of what he said were mistaken. Perhaps, the Stradivari violin Rembert found was not red. Tarisio #51374 remains a prime suspect for being the Stradivari violin Rembert identified around 1926.

Provenance

-	Rembert Wurlitzer Inc.
until 1968	Jacques Francais
from 1968	Current owner

Certificates & Documents

- Certificate: Jacques Francais, New York, NY (1968) *#929.*
- Certificate: Rembert Wurlitzer Inc., New York, NY

Screen shot of Tarisio #51374 Provenance

Tarisio Certificates and Documents are unavailable.

Chapter 4

Rembert's Discovery of a Stradivari Violin

The story I have often repeated how Rembert found a red Stradivarious violin seemed to me as a youth interesting, but not world-shaking. My father's narration, which was not the least bit hearsay, was direct confirmation of how Rembert discovered a red Stradivarius violin. I believe completely in the story's authenticity, at least to the extent Rembert identified a Stradivari violin in the mid 1920's.

The timeline for Rembert's discovery suggests it was between 1925 and 1928. The violin may have been entered briefly into the Wurlitzer inventory, but I doubt that too because at the time of discovery, he was not working for Wurlitzer. If there was an entry in Wurlitzer inventory, and that inventory was recovered, there would be a date. He did not start working for Wurlitzer until 1926. My best guess is that he found his Stradivari violin shortly before working for Wurlitzer. The incident almost certainly took place in the 1920s before my father left Wurlitzer in 1928.

One can reasonably speculate that Rembert's appointment to be in charge of Wurlitzer acquisitions in 1926 was in part to make sure he did not work for W.H. Hill who had offered him a job. Secondly, one can assume the Wurlitzer Board was impressed with Rembert's discovery of a rare Stradivarius violin. Rembert's knowledge and expertise was very apparent. His find of a rare, red violin surely impressed the Board enough for them to consider making him their master of acquisitions.

This appointment created an odd corporate structure where Rembert became head of acquisitions over his father Rudolph. It is easiest to explain this appointment as a reward to Rembert for not having accepted a job offer from Alfred Hill and as recognition that Rembert had proven his skills at acquisitions by having acquired until then an unknown red Stradivarius violin. Time would prove their assessment of Rembert's skills to be well founded.

Rembert Wurlitzer (1904–1963)
Probably in the late 1920s

Chapter 5

Another Mystery: Why was the Red Violin not Entered into the Wurlitzer and Rembert's Inventory?

Marianne, the daughter of Rembert, wrote to me on 4/2/2020 that she did not recall that her father had handled (or owned or held on consignment) *The Mendelssohn*. Her assertion seemed to be an existential threat to my book, *The Real Red Violin: A True Story About Rembert, the "Stradivarius Wurlitzer."* I became depressed. Surely, if Rembert had found a red Stradivarius violin as my father related that was *The Mendelssohn*, why was it not listed in any inventory?

The Mendelssohn is not listed by Goodkind as having been in a Wurlitzer inventory. How could this be? Although I knew the Goodkind and Tarisio records were incomplete, *The Mendelssohn* was certainly in one Wurlitzer inventory or another at one time – or if not in an inventory, it, or an unaccounted red violin, had been in Rembert's possession. I had the advantage over others knowing what my father had told me – Rembert had found an unnamed red violin in Berlin. My task was to show that the red violin was indeed *The Mendelssohn*.

Goodkind's and Rembert's records were obviously incomplete. Then it occurred to me that Rembert had owned the *The Mendelssohn* when he did not know for sure it was *The Mendelssohn*. It would have been listed briefly, possibly in an original Wurlitzer Music Company inventory, as simply an unnamed Stradivarius of 1720. That is how Tarisio lists the violin as number 51374. That listing probably reflects the original Wurlitzer listing. Tarisio never amended the listing.

But Rembert may not have put his red violin in even the Wurlitzer inventory if he found it and bought it before he worked for Wurlitzer. It was his violin, not Wurlitzer's. It would have been inappropriate to list it in Wurlitzer inventory. If he sold it for more than what he paid for it, he would have kept the profits unless instructed to do otherwise.

This scenario suggested strongly Rembert found his red violin in 1926 or the year before. One of the reasons I felt he had been hired to be head of Wurlitzer acquisitions in 1926 was based upon his proven expertise in finding this red Stradivarius.

Later in 1956, when Rembert bought *The Mendelssohn* from Hamma, he did know the provenance better, but he did not list it in his inventory presumably for personal reasons. In the play that follows, I speculate what those reasons may have been. Basically, he felt the red violin was a "keeper" not to be placed in an inventory of violins awaiting sale.

This absence in listing strongly suggests Rembert obscured, hid, or did not acknowledge ownership of *The Mendelssohn* or some Stradivari in his inventory, leading Goodkind, Tarisio, and his daughter Marianne to assert Rembert had not owned *The Mendelssohn*. Rembert may have left *The Mendelssohn* unnamed originally as the provenance for Tarisio #51374 strongly suggests, or he simply did not enter it into any inventory.

Both Goodkind and Tarisio did not recognize that Rembert had found a red Stradivari violin. Identifying the real red violin Rembert found has not been an easy task. I am now almost convinced that the red violin my father told me Rembert discovered was indeed *The Mendelssohn*.

I surmise that Rembert did not enter his purchase of *The Mendelssohn* in 1956 into his inventory, because the violin was a "keeper" holding special meaning to him. Tarisio records suggest he kept this violin until his death in 1963.

Freddie Beare, whose father worked for Wurlitzer, wrote in a private email in July 2020, "I've done some digging in the Wurlitzer database and found an instrument that matches the "*Mendelssohn*." Mr. Beare may be correct. If his supposition is incorrect, I surmise that Rembert purposely kept the violin out of inventory of instruments meant to be sold. The violin was a keeper as much as his wedding ring, never to be sold.

Admittedly, this rationale for not listing the violin is speculation, but it is speculation based on history as presented in the play that follows called simply *Rembert*.

Chapter 6

Pros and Cons Regarding the Argument that Rembert Found a Red Stradivarius Violin around 1926 that Turned Out to Be *The Mendelssohn.*

PROS:

A. Raimund Wurlitzer, the author's father, related several times to the author that Rembert had found a red Stradivarius violin in an outdoor cafe in Berlin. Raimund never gave a year. Although this testimony is now hearsay, the author gives the Raimund story complete support as being truthful at least to Rembert having identified a Stradivari in a Berlin café presumably around 1926. It is possible that my father's recollection the violin was red and my exact memory of what my father said are incorrect.

B. The Tarisio records for the "Unnamed" Stradivarius of 1720 Tarisio #51374 cites Rembert as the first owner. This "unnamed" Stradivarius could be *The Mendelssohn,* except it is not red.

C. *The Mendelssohn* and *The Unnamed* are not the same violin despite both being Stradivari of 1720. Their records cannot be legitimately combined and supplemented by Goodkind's records for *The Mendelssohn.*

D. The Fulton provenance for *The Mendelssohn* is incomplete from 1913 until 1920. The Fulton Provenance adds nothing to the provenance of this fiddle. Complete Wurlitzer records are unavailable.

E. The Fulton/Rembert/Wurlitzer database carries no overt entries for *The Mendelssohn,* because in the author's opinion Rembert did not intend to sell the fiddle. However, Mr. Fulton wrote that he would not be surprised if the stock card for the Wurlitzer Stradivari of 1720 was *The Mendelssohn.*

Alternatively that reference could have been for the "unnamed" Stradivari, otherwise known as Tarisio #51374. That violin appears in comparing the backs of Goodkind photos to be possibly *The Comte de Villares of 1720.* It is likely that Goodkind does not list *The Unnamed.* I could not find a Stradivari of 1720 back in Goodkind's book that matched closely the back of Tarisio #51734.

F. The lack of entry of *The Mendelssohn* into Rembert's records and Wurlitzer records, obtainable or presently unobtainable, can be explained. When Rembert found the fiddle, he was not working for Wurlitzer. Later he considered the fiddle a "keeper" as indicated by the Tarisio record showing he kept *The Mendelssohn* from 1956 until he died in 1963.

G. Personal testimony of Freddie Beare suggests there was *The Mendelssohn* or at least a violin like *The Mendelssohn* in Rembert's records, although Marianne, the daughter of Rembert does not recall *The Mendelssohn.* However, she did not work for her father. She worked instead for her mother Lee after her father's death. Accordingly, she had less exposure to her father's thoughts than she would have had she worked for her father.

H. Rembert's appointment to be head of acquisitions for Wurlitzer in

1926 at an extraordinarily young age reflected in part, I speculate, an appreciation by the Wurlitzer Board for Rembert having found earlier a previously undescribed red Stradivarius violin. This unusual appointment put Rembert allegedly above his experienced father Rudolph creating an odd corporate structure where a relatively unexperienced Rembert was a titular superior to his father in acquisitions.

This odd structure might be best explained as a reward to Rembert for having found a Stradivarius violin and to discourage him from accepting a job offer from Alfred Hill who was also impressed with Rembert for having found a red Stradivarius violin. It is awkward to explain this Wurlitzer job offer in any other way. Wurlitzer corporate records surrounding Rembert's appointment are unavailable.

I. Historically, dealer records and provenances are often incomplete, because of concerns that privacy and confidentiality be kept. A lack of evidence from examining records proves nothing.

J. There is absolutely no proof yet that the red Stradivarius Rembert found was not *The Mendelssohn.* The absence of proof that Rembert did not find *The Mendelssohn* is no proof under American and English common law precedents that he did not find it.

K. Regarding the argument that Rembert did not buy rare musical instruments, he obviously did from time to time, as for example, the Henry Hottinger collection in 1967. At the time I allege Rembert found his red Stradivari violin, he was not working for Wurlitzer. He was not a dealer then.

L. Regarding the argument Francesco Mendelssohn sold *The Mendelssohn* sometime after 1913 when he was an owner, there is no record of a sale that has been found. Most likely, Francesco lost *The*

Mendelssohn in Berlin. It was later in Berlin that my father reported Rembert identified a red Stradivarius.

M. It is conjecture that Herr Hamma felt morally obligated to sell *The Mendelssohn* to Rembert, because Rembert had sold it to him.

CONS:

A. Tarisio records are notoriously inaccurate or incomplete.

B. Rembert did not buy rare musical instruments. He only took them on consignment as a dealer. That claim is not true as evidenced by the purchase of the Henry Hottinger collection in 1967 and other purchases too numerous to cite.

C. There are no conclusive records proving or disproving the argument Rembert found *The Mendelssohn*. The absence of records of *The Mendelssohn* in the Fulton/Rembert database tends to disprove (in the eyes of those not legally trained) that Rembert possessed *The Mendelssohn*.

Summmary of Pros and Cons

The mystery has not been conclusively solved in my opinion. While unequivocal proof has not been presented that the red Stradivarius violin Rembert found was *The Mendelssohn*, the circumstantial evidence is strong. That Rembert kept *The Mendelssohn* for the rest of his life after purchasing it in 1956 appears to be a fact. That prolonged ownership is convincing evidence *The Mendelssohn* had special meaning for him.

That Rembert identified a Stradivari violin around the mid 1920s in a Berlin café is a fact in my mind. But whether or not it was *The Red Mendelssohn,* I cannot definitely conclude. In my mind, it probably was *The Mendelssohn*, although *The Unnamed* is still a suspect.

I have facetiously considered seeking a court order to rule in favor of the argument that Rembert found *The Mendelssohn*. It would be entertaining I feel to attach a court order to this book. What fully happened around the time of Rembert's discovery is in part speculation, so I decided to make it into a play relating what I think happened.

Chapter 7

The Very Entertaining Francesco Mendelssohn.

The Fulton provenance, Appendix 2, page 153, lists Francesco Mendelssohn as an owner of *The Mendelssohn* in 1913. Who was this man other than knowing he was the great nephew of Felix Mendelssohn, the great composer? How did *The Mendelssohn* get from his hands into those of Rembert? The play, *Rembert*, attempts to answer these questions.

Francesco Mendelssohn was such a fascinating and important character in the history of *The Mendelssohn* violin that I find it worthwhile to be repetitive in driving the point home that in my opinion, he lost the violin. The reader may fairly ask how anyone could lose a rare musical instrument. Be assured that Francesco was a professional at losing instruments.

Francesco Mendelssohn was a confirmed alcoholic. But he was also a brave and forgetful alcoholic. Rembert knew him well. Francesco has become a very entertaining character in the play.

Francesco's father was a nephew of composer Felix Mendelssohn. In a bizarre turn of fate, Francesco purchased *The Mendelssohn*, a violin his great uncle Felix had owned from Wilhelm Hermann Hammig in 1913. Sometime after 1913, I speculate

Francesco lost *The Mendelssohn* in a drunken stupor. The circumstantial evidence is impressive that this mishap occurred.

One-time in the late 1930's, Francesco smuggled his famous Stradivarius *Piatti cello* across the border from Germany into Switzerland on his bicycle. From Switzerland he went to New York where he met Rembert.[14]

Often Francesco would leave *the Piatti* in bars as ways of settling tabs. He may have told Rembert later that he didn't smuggle *The Mendelssohn*, because as in our play the author speculates Francesco had lost that violin years earlier. After all, *The Mendelssohn* was more valuable in the late 1930's than the *Piatti Cello*, so surely he would have smuggled *The Mendelssohn* rather than the Piatti. He had no room on his bicycle for two instruments. It is a fact Francesco smuggled the *Piatti*. Why not *The Mendelssohn*? What happened to *The Mendelssohn* after 1913 when records show Francesco had owned it?

It is true Francesco may have sold *The Mendelssohn* sometime after 1913, but it was not in his character to sell Stradivari. He was better at losing them. The history is clear he had lost two instruments due to negligence.

It is well reported that one night after a concert in New York around 1950, Francesco tried to enter his home on East 62nd St. He became frustrated. He was unable to open his front door. Awakening to the fact that being in an alcoholic stupor that he was at the wrong house, he left his cello on the footpath as he staggered off to his own home.[15]

The next morning his housekeeper awoke him and asked if a cello she has found on the street was his. "I found it in the street, just as the

---

[14] Adventures of a Cello by Carlos Prieto. University of Texas Press. 2006
[15] Ibid.

garbage truck was about to pick it up," she said. Francesco may not have even thanked her.[16]

A second episode occurred according to Freddie Beare [17] who had worked for years for Wurlitzer when Francesco planned to take a trip with his *Red Piatti Stradivarius*. Knowing how unreliable and untrustworthy Francesco was with musical instruments, Rembert insisted that Francesco take a cello Rembert had made years earlier in Mirecourt. Francesco agreed. Then the dwelling Francesco was in caught fire, some speculated from Francesco dropping lighted cigarettes in a drunken stupor, destroying the cello and the dwelling. But a precious Stradivarius had been saved.

It is the author's well-founded speculation that Francesco didn't dare tell anyone, about a similar episode in 1913. After a concert he became alarmingly inebriated. I venture, that foolishly, Francesco left *The Mendelssohn* on the street before his home in Germany, as he had the Piatti. A garbage collector that time picked up the violin and later sold it to a gypsy.

Francesco was apparently indifferent to leaving Stradivari instruments on streets for garbage collectors or in bars to assure later payments. Arguably, he left the violin on the Berlin street to assure the garbage collectors he would pay them.

In any event, he didn't complain to authorities in Germany then in 1913, because he was Jewish. Maybe, he didn't complain partly, because he had been utterly besotted and stupid. Who would sympathize with a stupid, frequently besotted Jew in an anti-Semetic Germany? In France, the military officer Dreyfus was sent to Devil's Island for being Jewish. What could Mendelssohn expect in sympathy for being Jewish and stupid?

---

[16] https://www.irishtimes.com/culture/memoirs-of-a-stradivarius-1.932980
[17] This story was related to me by Mr. David Fulton.

Francesco also enjoyed not just leaving Stradivari instruments in bars to assure later payment, but rather pawning Stradivari instruments in bars to pay for alcohol and then buying them back later. That casual never-do-well attribute for handling rare musical instruments no doubt seemed entertaining to many -- and he was a charmer -- but it was hard on rare instruments in his possession. It is even partially understandable, since Strads weren't as monetarily valuable back then as they are today.

Francesco was not a salesman; he was a drinker and terminator of musical instruments. It is miraculous his *Piatti* survived.

It may be also that no concert cellists ever wanted to loan Francesco an instrument, although he was an excellent cellist. "Buyer beware" became "player beware" in his presence. Sometimes, before a concert if he had misplaced an instrument, it is doubtful any musician would loan him one.

In a further bizarre twist of fate, I hazard that very same gypsy, who bought *The Mendelssohn* from a Berlin trash collector, played the Chaconne for Rembert and Raimund in an outdoor Berlin café in 1926.

In appreciation, after of course another round of drinks, Francesco, I like to think, later called Rembert, "The Resurrector of *The Mendelssohn*." Then the instrument was in Rembert's reliable hands, and especially so when many years later it was sold to Mr. Pitcairn who gave it to his daughter Elizabeth.

When I met Rembert three times in Manhattan with my father when I was a lad, I wish I had asked him which violin my father said he had discovered. I wish my father had asked too, but the movie *The Red Violin* was yet to be made. *The Red Violin* name had little, if any meaning to me, my father, or possibly even Rembert back then, although in my immediate Wurlitzer household lore there had been a red violin that Rembert had discovered.

Rembert
A PLAY

Introduction
To the Play

In the book *Rembert* I presented a brief history of the Wurlitzer family and that of Rembert with arguments supporting the thesis that a red violin my father witnessed Rembert discovering was *The Mendelssohn*. A summary of those arguments is presented again here as an independent introduction to the play. Following that I present a play relating more thoroughly what I think is the true story of *The Mendelssohn* from the time just before Rembert found it to the time of Rembert's death.

One of the main characters in the play, *Rembert*, is Francesco Mendelssohn, the great-nephew of the composer Felix Mendelssohn. Francesco was a master cellist and a master at losing rare musical cellos. He was also a master alcoholic, not a Meistersinger, but a "Meisterweiner," or if you will a "Meistertrinker."

Fulton database records presented in the book later show Francesco was the owner of a rare Stradivarius violin called *The Mendelssohn* in 1913. There is no record of Francesco having sold this violin.

In the late 1930s, Francesco smuggled his famous Stradivarius *Piatti Cello* across Germany's border into Switzerland on his bicycle. From Switzerland he went to New York where he met Rembert. An relevant question is, why hadn't Francesco smuggled *The Mendelssohn* out of Germany?

Carlos Prieto records that Francesco would often leave *The Piatti* in bars as ways of settling tabs. This play proposes he didn't smuggle out *The Mendelssohn* that he owned in 1913, because he had lost it earlier. After all, *The Mendelssohn* was more valuable than the *Piatti Cello*. Surely, he would have smuggled *The Mendelssohn* rather than the *Piatti*. He had no room on his bicycle for two instruments, so why didn't he smuggle *The Mendelssohn*?

It is a fact Francesco smuggled the *Piatti*. Why not *The Mendelssohn*? What happened to *The Mendelssohn* after 1913 when records show Francesco had owned it?

It is possible Francesco may have sold *The Mendelssohn* sometime after 1913, but it was not in his character to sell Stradivari. Nor is there a record he sold *The Mendelssohn*.

Francesco was accomplished at losing rare musical instruments. Records show clearly he had lost two instruments due to negligence, so why not a third? It was part of his character to be indifferent to possessing rare musical instruments.

From the *Irish Times*: Memoirs of a Stradivarius Piatti Cello. Jan 29, 2008. *Irish Times*, "Known as the '*Red Cello*' because of its warmly glowing varnish, the *Piatti Cello* was made in 1720 – around the time when Bach was writing his six extraordinary suites for unaccompanied cello. Besides the *Piatti*, the 76-year-old master luthier from Cremona, Antonio Stradivari, produced 14 violins that year. It took him just over a month to make the cello from Balkan maple and Italian pine."

"In another picaresque twist, the cello ended up in Nazi Germany in the hands of Francesco Mendelssohn, whose father was a nephew of composer Felix Mendelssohn. He managed to smuggle it across the border into Switzerland – on his bicycle – and thence to New York. Sadly, once there, he went into a downward spiral of alcoholism; with some hair-raising results for the *Piatti*, which was often left behind in bars by way of settling the tab."

"One night after a concert, Mendelssohn had a few scoops too many and, on getting out of a taxi on East 62nd Street, was unable to open his own front door. Gradually it dawned on him that he was at the wrong house. Leaving the cello case on the footpath, he staggered off in search of the right one. Next morning he woke to hear his housekeeper declaring, 'Isn't this your cello? I found it lying in the street just as the garbage truck was about to pick it up?'

A second episode occurred according to Freddie Beare, who had worked for years for Wurlitzer when Francesco planned to take a trip with his *Red Piatti Stradivarius*. Knowing how unreliable and untrustworthy Francesco was with musical instruments, Rembert insisted that Francesco take a cello Rembert had made years earlier in Mirecourt. Francesco agreed. Then the dwelling Francesco was in caught fire, some speculated from Francesco dropping lighted cigarettes in a drunken stupor, destroying the cello and the dwelling. But a precious Stradivarius had been saved, while another instrument had been lost.

I speculate that Francesco had a similar episode in 1913 losing *The Mendelssohn*. After a concert, I suggest Francesco became, as usual, alarmingly inebriated. Then I suggest he left *The Mendelssohn* again as he had once earlier left the *Piatti* on the street before his home in Germany. Then I suggest a garbage collector picked up the violin and later sold it to a gypsy.

Why do I say a gypsy? My father recalled he and Rembert had agreed it was probably a gypsy who played the red Stradivarius Rembert identified.

Understandably, after losing his Stradivarius, I suggest Francesco didn't complain to authorities in Germany then in 1913, because he was Jewish. Maybe, he didn't complain because he had been utterly besotted and stupid. Being a besotted, stupid Jew might have gained him as much sympathy as Dreyfus did around the same time in France.

Francesco also enjoyed not just leaving Stradivari instruments in bars to assure later payment, but rather pawning Stradivari instruments in bars to pay for alcohol and then buying them back later. That casual, ne'er-do-well attribute for handling rare musical instruments no doubt seemed entertaining to many – and he was a charmer – but he was hard on rare instruments in his possession.

Francesco was a threat to precious musical instruments. He was by all accounts entertaining, but dangerous when musical instruments were in his possession.

The Piatti was red and was known as the "*Red Cello.*" So is *The Red Mendelssohn*. Maybe, Francesco just didn't like to see red. Perhaps, he became red in the face when he saw red. Maybe, unconscioiusly he always wanted to make red disappear when he saw it. I am just speculating in a manner many psychiatrists do about others.

"Buyer beware!" became "Player beware!" in Francesco's presence. Sometimes, before a concert if he had misplaced an instrument, it was doubtful any musician would loan him one.

In a further bizarre twist of fate, I suggest that very same gypsy, who bought *The Mendelssohn* from a Berlin trash collector, played the Chaconne for Rembert and my father Raimund in an outdoor Berlin café in 1926.

In appreciation, after, of course, another round of drinks, Francesco, I like to think, later called Rembert, "The Resurrector of *The Mendelssohn.*" Then, the instrument was in Rembert's reliable hands, and as well, many years later, it was again in reliable hands when it came into the possession of Elizabeth Pitcairn.

I feel privileged that I knew most of the 20th century characters in this book.

Plot and Scenes

The story starts with Rembert and his dad, Rudolph, in an office (Scene #1). They talk about Stradivari violins' beauty and the remarkable 300-year family history (today, it is a 400-year history) of making musical instruments.

Scenes #2 through #5 are at an outdoor Berlin café where Rembert first identifies an unknown red violin.

Scenes #6 and #7 are, like Scene #1, located in an office. There are then virtually just two set designs.

Rembert is shown as a gifted young man who is infatuated and obsessed with rare violins. Fortunately, he discovers a red Stradivarius that, in the play, becomes a significant focus of his life. His father forces him to sell it. He recovers it; he hides it; he then possesses it again, and again hiding it until he dies. The violin became a secret obsession.

Raimund, a character in this play, is the author's father, and Rembert is the first cousin once removed of the author. Howard is the grandfather of the author and CEO, while Rudolph is the great uncle of the author and head of the rare instruments department. Rudolph, Howard, and Farny are brothers of Franz Rudolph, the founder of the Wurlitzer Music Company. The author feels free to write about his father, Rembert, and his wife Lee since they have all died.

Family Tree

To help the audience understand relationships, a family tree follows that outlines the filial relations of the principal characters in this mostly true-to-life play.

This outline can be put in the program. The author apologizes for the convoluted family connections, although they are what they are.

Wurlitzer Family Tree (Characters acted in Play are highlighted in bold capitals)

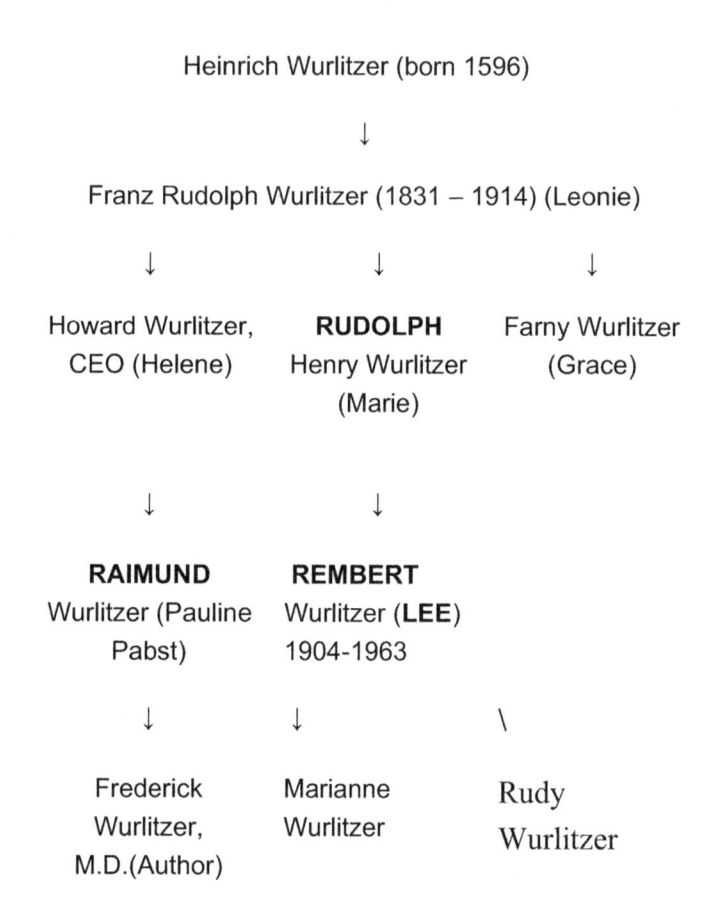

Heinrich Wurlitzer (born 1596)
↓
Franz Rudolph Wurlitzer (1831 – 1914) (Leonie)
↓   ↓   ↓

| Howard Wurlitzer, CEO (Helene) | **RUDOLPH** Henry Wurlitzer (Marie) | Farny Wurlitzer (Grace) |

↓   ↓

| **RAIMUND** Wurlitzer (Pauline Pabst) | **REMBERT** Wurlitzer (**LEE**) 1904-1963 |

↓   ↓   \

| Frederick Wurlitzer, M.D.(Author) | Marianne Wurlitzer | Rudy Wurlitzer |

Henry Farny, the renowned Western painter, was the brother of Leonie, the wife of Franz Joseph, the Wurlitzer founder.

This play follows logical speculations about what conversations took place over time by the author's family members a long time ago, so, it is not entirely a fairy tale. Mostly what is depicted is based on facts as the author could find them looking at databases, reading numerous books, and communicating with relatives and associates.

There are Wurlitzers making music instruments still today. That equates to there being now over a remarkable, four-hundred-year lineage of Wurlitzer musical instrument-making. How one might explain this longevity in focus is another theme. The American Wurlitzer Music Company itself is out of business, although there is a Deutsche Wurlitzer making instruments in Hűllhorst, Germany.

The author is a black sheep who decided to become a physician instead of becoming a Wurlitzer instrument maker. There was a brief period, though, when he appointed a surrogate to the Wurlitzer Board.

In writing the play, characters start speaking a few words in German. The use of German is meant to add authenticity to the principals' well-defined German ancestry and pervasive German business relations.

In writing a play or a book, a dedication or an acknowledgment is appropriate. Without the benefit of having been confined because of the Coronavirus, I would never have had the patience and focus to write this story. I would have just had another glass of red wine and mused about my past failures. This is the author's first play.

Characters

Principal Characters

- **REMBERT**, a famous American violin collector and dealer;
- **RUDOLPH** Henry, Rembert's father and also a famous American expert in rare violins;
- **HERR HAMMA,** a well-known German violin dealer and Wurlitzer colleague in Stuttgart;
- **RAIMUND**, the first cousin of Rembert;
- **LEE**, Rembert's wife;
- **FRANCESCO,** grand nephew of Felix Mendelssohn.

Minor Characters

- **GYPSY,** who plays a red violin to recorded music;
- **REPORTER,** a newspaper reporter for the Music Times.

Note: One actor plays **HERR HAMMA**, and the **GYPSY**. Another actor plays the **REPORTER and FRANCESCO**. Different actors play **REMBERT**, **RUDOLPH**, and **RAIMUND**. One actress will play **LEE**. There are a total of eight characters, but possibly only six actors, depending upon how the director assigns roles.

Opening

The actor or character playing Francesco Mendelssohn enters, faces the audience, and states his thoughts. He is dressed as a Jew with a *yarmulke* – and he is drinking from a bottle of whiskey labeled in bold letters "WHISKEY."

FRANCESCO I am Francesco Mendelssohn; I am truly a clod. My great uncle, Felix, was truly a genius. I am just an ordinary genius. Uncle Felix was not a clod. I am a clod. Felix's music was glorious, almost as ethereal as the music of Bach. I am not just a clod; I am a drunken fool. I've lost Felix's violin, *The Mendelssohn*. Felix would play the Chaconne on it. It was heaven opening its heart to all men. I am leaving to have another drink. Have no pity on me. What will I do without my red violin?

[Francesco staggers off the stage when he finishes his sad opening soliloquy.]

SCENE #1

A den filled with books and violins where Rudolph is sitting behind a desk. A sign high above the desk says, "Wurlitzer Music Company" and immediately below that there is "Cincinnati." The year is 1922 when Rembert is 18 years old.

[Rembert knocks on the door]

RUDOLPH Come in.

[Rembert enters.]

You're late. Still, it's good to see you, son. Sit down, please. Have you been enjoying Cincinnati? Your mother and I missed you today.

REMBERT Yes, Dad, I enjoyed my time in New York visiting dealers, but I missed Mom and you too.

RUDOLPH You just got back home, and we didn't see you. What did you do today that was so important that you couldn't have spent time first with us?

REMBERT I went to the Cincinnati Art Museum to see my Uncle Henry Farny's paintings again. He really was a great Western artist, better in my mind than Remington or Russell. He didn't care what people thought of him. He only cared about painting. He told me it was important to do what you like. "Be your own guide. Look for beauty; only do what you want," he told me. Those words became implanted in my soul. I miss him and his simplicity and purity of focus. Someday, I may be able to say what people think of me does not matter. Someday, I may even be able to do only what I want.

RUDOLPH Don't distract me. You are 18. It's time you to go to University. Most importantly, how are you doing?

REMBERT I wasn't trying to distract you. Before you even asked me what I wanted to do, I told you. I knew you really didn't care what I wanted. You want me to go to university. I don't. I want to study violins. I want to find beauty. You want me to squeeze me into your mold of whom I should be.

RUDOLPH You're certainly abrupt and to the point. Why is there always tension between us?

[A pause as Rudolph reflects]

Son, you have always been very special to me, not just because you are my only son, but because of your love for violins. That

	love reminds me of myself. You must go to university and then come and work with Howard and me. Then, you can
	pursue your love affair of fine violins. How you developed that love, I'm not sure.
REMBERT	It was from you, Dad, that I developed my love for violins. You were an excellent violinist yourself. You even studied under Emanuel Wirth in Berlin for almost a year. Your deep love for rare violins somehow struck a musical chord in my soul. I just responded with love myself, almost as strong as my love for my mother. We share a love for the beauty of rare violins and Mom.
RUDOLPH	Those are wonderful sentiments.
REMBERT	Dad, I really appreciate your kindness and support, but I just do not see how university will help me. I wonder what I will learn and if what I learn will help me. I love violins and playing them more than I do women. I just want to know everything about them like you. I'm pissed that I have to go to Princeton.
RUDOLPH	University will help you broaden your knowledge. It will introduce you to new ideas, maybe even different women other than your mom.

REMBERT You didn't go to university and neither did your brothers Farny and Howard. My grandfather Franz Rudolph thought university was a waste of time, and so did you. I really don't like being forced to do what none of my family did. Why are you hurting me?

RUDOLPH I am just thinking what is best for you. I regret now I didn't go to university. I understand your feelings, even if I do not sympathize with your priorities like going to the art museum here in Cincinnati before seeing your mother and me. I insist you go to university. Let's have no more talk that you won't go.

REMBERT I regret I didn't see Mom first. But how could I have seen Mom without seeing you? You are putting me in a can. You're squeezing me into a tube. I feel like I am in a vise. You are tormenting me.

RUDOLPH You're mixing metaphors, son.

REMBERT To hell with mixed metaphors! Please try to understand me. I guess I was blessed, or maybe cursed, with an orientation that violins are the greatest. I even think more about violins than I do about women and sex, or even Mom.

RUDOLPH Maybe, my friend Sigmund Freud would say you have a fetish or a lust for violins. After all, violins have hourglass figures. He would say if you

understood your dreams, you would understand yourself better.

REMBERT Really?

RUDOLPH Yes, really! I can arrange an appointment with Herr Freud if you are even a little bit interested. I consider him a friend. As you apparently know, Sigmund played music on a Wurlitzer piano. I sold one to him a while back. He played it for me in his home on Bergasse not far from our home on Wurlitzergasse in Vienna. You may be amused that I once told him I dreamed of violins, but he just smiled and said nothing more. So, I prefer not saying anything more. I don't think Freud wanted to challenge me, since he wanted to buy one of our pianos.

REMBERT How anyone would see my love for violins as being erotic is beyond my understanding, I just dream of their beauty.

RUDOLPH Hah, in my opinion your love for violins is indeed erotic. Otherwise, you'd dream of naked women rather than naked violins.

Don't patronize me, son. I don't like your tone of resentment.

REMBERT How is what you like relevant to my needs?

RUDOLPH You need to accept our proud history of making musical instruments for hundreds of years.

REMBERT *[Delivered angrily]*

Why do I need to accept that history? Dad, I can't explain the mystery of a family focus for hundreds of years being involved one way or another with music. Maybe psychiatric illnesses are passed down genetically from one generation to the next. Some genetic illnesses like hemophilia are certainly passed down for generations. Maybe, love-hate relationships between father and son are passed down culturally through generations. I recall Franz Rudolph, who founded our company, was divorced by his father Christian Gottfried. Christian passed the business in East Germany to his youngest, only six-year-old son, Constatin. Franz Rudolph bitterly resented what his father had done. Now I bitterly feel you are disinheriting me. You're pushing me to leave rare violins, although violins came first in your life. I would rather be with violins than with you or in University. Maybe disinheritance will flow from son to father this time around.

RUDOLPH You're insulting. I am having trouble holding back my anger. It's curious though that Freud suggested to me I had a lust for violins as you apparently have. But remember please everyone in our family fell in love with music

one way or another. Everyone sought beauty somehow in what they did. I would be very pleased if you sought beauty in violins as I once did.

REMBER *[Again, delivered angrily]*

Maybe, each father affected every son by example. It then became the son's choice whether or not to follow the father. I don't know, and I don't care.

RUDOLPH Be patient, son. Answers will emerge.

REMBERT Are you kidding? Be patient. Excuse me, what nonsense!

RUDOLPH Why are you so angry?

REMBERT Maybe, you should talk to a psychiatrist to find out. Maybe, I should too.

RUDOLPH You have so much to be proud about. Don't you feel pride? Our company makes the Mighty Wurlitzer organs for movie theaters, and automated orchestrions and other automated musical instruments. Our name means music to millions of Americans with whom we have relationships. I feel pride. Why don't you?

	After university, you can go back to violins or even if you want, only women. Please understand
	I am asking you to consider priorities.
REMBERT	Dad, I'm tired and ready to check out. Your price means little to me.
RUDOLPH	Am I boring you?
REMBERT	Yes, you were boring me except when you mentioned the Mighty Wurlitzer organ. Speaking of that, I've had a "Mighty Wurlitzer organ" all my life.
RUDOLPH	Smart ass!

[as he lowers his head and chuckles fondly]

	Just don't be rude with others who might be less patient than I am when you talk about your "mighty organ." You've really tested my patience.
REMBERT	*[Rembert is really a spoiled brat lecturing his father.]*
	And you have tested my patience. Frankly, I feel I have more patience than you. Pushing me to do what I don't want to do does not impress me as being a virtue indicating patience.
RUDOLPH	You act like a spoiled brat.
REMBERT	And you act like an overbearing German father.

SCENE #2

A four-year time lapse takes place. The year is 1926

Background: Goebbels was sent by Hitler in October 1926 to the German capital, Berlin, to be its Gauleiter. The police declared the Nazi Party illegal in Berlin and eventually banned Nazi speech throughout the entire German state of Prussia.

Lights are dimmed as an outdoor café is set up.

An outdoor café in Berlin, Germany in 1926. A sign says in German, "*Wir feiern 1926 mit Bier.*" (We celebrate 1926 with beer.) Raimund and Rembert are drinking beer.

RAIMUND *Wie geht's mein Vetter?* How are you doing, my cousin? It's been four years since I last saw you just before you left for Princeton. So much has happened, and the Nazi Party has just been banned, I hope forever.

REMBERT *Doch fein, Danke, und Prost!*

[...as Rembert lifts a stein of beer to Raimund who is also drinking beer, in fact, Pabst beer even though Pabst beer was usually unavailable in Germany at that time. The beer they are drinking can be labeled boldly "Pabst." They talk further in English.]

Very well, thank you, and *Prost*. Did you just get here? What are you doing here in Berlin? I'm just fine; I'm here because I was bloody tired of university. So, I came to Berlin to drink beer and learn. I even have time to think about women and sex – and yes, the Nazis are being put down, fortunately.

RAIMUND It's commendable that you would drink beer while thinking about women and sex, when not worrying about Nazis. My wife Pauline and I were already in Germany. We have just come from Markneukirchen and Vienna where we visited relatives. So, it was easy for us to see you. My wife is back at our hotel.

REMBERT I hope I can see Pauline later.

RAIMUND Thank you. Maybe, we can get together later. So, fill me in, please. What's been happening in your life?

REMBERT

Soliloquy #4 *[Related calmly]*

As you know, I dropped out of Princeton after two years. I couldn't take it anymore. My father was deeply disappointed, but I don't feel I was a failure as he seemed to think I was. I just wasn't learning what I wanted to know. I was tired of studying what I didn't want to learn. So,

I went to Europe, finally, at my father's suggestion after I had wasted two years. Here in Berlin, I visited numerous violin dealers and just talked with them about rare violins. It was illuminating. Actually, it was thrilling. I also went to France and Italy, where I studied violins and met violin dealers. Those two years were like a two-year postgraduate course in violins. Everyone welcomed me because of my father. No one wanted to talk about Nazis. I finally rationalized my anger at being made to go to university. I forgave my father.

RAIMUND How did your father make you go to university?

REMBERT He made it clear I better conform, or he wouldn't let me work with him later at Wurlitzer. It was extortion.

RAIMUND I know what you mean being upset with your father. My father, Howard was very dominating with me. He made me go to university also. I didn't want to go. But I met my wife at university. So, it worked out okay. Howard insisted I do this and that, like going to his spy school where he tested my memory. He would take me into a pub, leave, and then demand to know who had been in the bar, how they were dressed, and what they were talking about listening from a distance. I inevitably failed. It was weird. He had other memory games. I resented them. Then, he demanded I work with him. I thought if I worked with him, he would abuse me more, and he did.

REMBERT Maybe, it's just a German thing to pressure children to carry on an inheritance.

RAIMUND My wife and I will try not to influence our children excessively to do what we think they should do.

REMBERT We have interesting parallels. Our histories are like two grape vines twisting together as they grow, waiting to be plucked by others.

RAIMUND Your father is very well known as an expert in rare violins. He has bought, authenticated, restored, and sold many, many Stradivari instruments. You can be proud of him, and I know him to be well-intentioned. My father was well-intentioned too, but overbearing and impatient with incompetency. He thought I was incompetent.

REMBERT Yes, my father helped me tremendously with contacts. In England, I worked and studied with the very important English dealer and scholar, Mr. W.H. Hill. My father has worked often with Mr. Hill. Now I just want to go back home to work in the violin department of our company.

RAIMUND I hope when you return you don't feel you are

entering enemy territory controlled by your father. We know that your father and you had disagreements. Howard will protect you. He sees you as a son, more, I think, than he does me.

[*A pause as Raimund reflects*]

Your father and Howard have tremendous admiration for you. Pauline and I were here anyway in Germany. At the urging of your dad and my dad, my mission became to talk with you. We are concerned that you may be so upset with your father that you do not return to Cincinnati.

REMBERT Don't be concerned. I am very pleased your wife and you are here.

RAIMUND Our friends and colleagues who are violin dealers in Berlin have already attested that you have a profound knowledge of and an unusual interest in rare violins. Mr. Hamma, our colleague, also attests to your abilities. Mr. Hill has confirmed your abilities. We think Mr. Hill may offer you a job and that you may accept.

REMBERT Thank you for your kind comments. What do you have in mind?

RAIMUND I am not just being kind; I am being truthful. We would very much welcome you back. Howard wants you. We run a major business that we expect will some day be on the New York Stock Exchange. We all recognize that we need someone like you. We want you to return home to be with us.

REMBERT What do Howard and my father say? What exactly would I do?

RAIMUND The Board concurs that you will work under your father who will provide you additional training. Consider what I'm saying as a job offer. We will talk about salary later, but you can be assured it will be fair.

REMBERT Thank you, Raimund. Mr. Hill has not offered me a job yet. So, don't be too concerned. I'll let you know after I talk with my dad. It's not just the money; it's the thought of being with beautiful violins that really excites me.

RAIMUND You have a sincere job offer. Do let us know soon if you are accepting the offer.

REMBERT My German is pretty good now. Shall we speak in German?

RAIMUND No, please. Let's continue to speak in English. Although my German is good, even still, I rarely have a chance to use it. After all my years in Cincinnati, I am now much more fluent in English. Learning German can be of great help, though, to a Wurlitzer. The Board did want to

	know how proficient you are in German, so we'll talk later *auf Deutsch*, my first language.
REMBERT	I know German is important to be working for Wurlitzer, and I have been diligent. I can be of great help with our colleagues and relatives in Germany. I have met Fritz Wurlitzer, our "Clarinet Wurlitzer" in Erlbach, and Herr Hamma in Stuttgart several times. I can help consolidate professional relations and not just family connections here in Germany.
RAIMUND	There is no doubt it really helps getting around Germany and Austria to speak fluent German. Our German connections are profound.
REMBERT	I also want to say that I appreciate and respect that you have come to Germany in large part just to offer me a job.
RAIMUND	Yes, but we did not come to Germany just to see you. Remember, please, we have relatives in Vienna on Wurlitzergasse. I was in you Schöneck, and of course Markneukirchen, and then Vienna earlier seeing other relatives and associates in the music business.

[A gypsy begins playing Bach's Chaconne outside where Raimund and Rembert are sitting.]

REMBERT Stop talking, Raimund, for a moment, please. Do you hear that gypsy playing a violin?

RAIMUND Yes, of course. But so what? That's the Chaconne, and he's playing it well.

REMBERT Hush! Listen!

[A five-second pause as Rembert listens raptly turning his head slowly side to side]

Oh, my God, I think he's playing a Stradivarius. I can't believe it.

RAIMUND Are you sure?

REMBERT Yes, I am almost sure. The sound is true, but I want to see the violin first before I am absolutely sure.

[Rembert goes up to the gypsy and politely asks…]

Hello mein Herr, darf Ich seine Geige ansehen? May I look at your violin?

GYPSY *[With a heavy German accent]*

Naturlich. Spielen Sie die Geige? Naturally, do you play the violin? [said with a leer reflecting sexual connotations]

REMBERT *Jawohl, Ich kann die Geige spielen.* Yes, I can play the violin, but I don't want to play your violin now. I just want to look at it. I think this is a very fine violin.

[Rembert looks intently at the violin turning it over several times, nodding his head up and down.]

I would like to buy it, please.

GYPSY No, I don't want to sell it. You just walk up, and announce you want to buy my violin? Then you say you want to look at and play my violin. Maybe, you were saying you want to play with my cock? You have *chutzpah* and big balls, my friend. But I will sell the violin to you anyway if you really have big balls for just $300. That's a bargain. I know you are American because of your *aussprache* or accent. And besides, all Americans have money. Do you have enough money?

REMBERT Okay, I'll give you 1200 rentenmark, or, if you wish, 300 dollars. I have enough dollars with me to pay you right now. Just give me a handwritten receipt. Don't ask to look at my balls to see how big they are.

GYPSY Okay, take the violin.

[The gypsy quickly scribbles out a receipt using

Rembert's pen on a piece of scrap paper.]

I'll go and buy some schnapps. That would be more enjoyable than talking with you further about your balls and you playing mine.

REMBERT *Geh mit Gott.* Go with God.

[Rembert goes back to the table outside the café.]

RAIMUND You just bought that violin? That was quick. It sure is red in color.

REMBERT Yes, I wanted it quick. That gypsy was very rude and crude – a real pain. Regarding the violin, I truly believe it's a red Stradivarius. I would like my father to authenticate it with me, then I can be absolutely sure. Anyway, it's a good violin, worth more than $300.

RAIMUND Getting your father involved might not be simple. He's in Cincinnati now. Let's go back to our hotels, and you can call him.

SCENE #3

Two weeks later, Rembert is again at the outdoor café, now with his father, Rudolph Henry. A sign is up as before, but now it just says "*Zwei Wochen später*" and underneath "Two weeks later." The year is still 1926.

Lights are dimmed and then turned up several times in the theater in order to accentuate this time-lapse of two weeks. The lights are red, of course, because this is a story, in part, about a red violin. Red is a color, also, for illicit sex. By the way, violins are not categorized by color.

REMBERT Did you have a good trip, Dad? Was the cruise to Warnemunde pleasant? I brought the red violin along so you can see it.

RUDOLPH Yes, I had a good cruise. Your mother is not with me. I dropped all matters and came to Berlin as quickly as I could after you told me you had found a red Stradivarius. I wanted to see you and the Stradivarius. And more importantly, I wanted to confirm Raimund's job offer and even more. Now the Board has decided to up our offer after your marvelous find of a red Straddivari violin. We would like you to head rare instrument purchases at Wurlitzer. Your appointment was based at first as a reaction to Mr. Hill's fondness of you and fear he might make you an offer. Based upon the expertise you showed finding a red Stradivarius, the Board is now anxious that you accept a job offer with us. We do not want to lose you to Mr. Hill, who we learned through the grape vine, made an offer to you two weeks ago.

REMBERT Thanks, Dad. Your offer means a lot to me, although I find it amusing Wurlitzer's greater interest in me now is related to my having found a red Stradivari violin and a wonderful job offer from Mr. Hill. I regret if my leaving Princeton upset you. I will seriously consider the new job offer.

RUDOLPH Son, I am no longer offended you dropped out of university. Let me make it clear that the offer is now for you to head acquisitions at Wurlitzer. You would be over me in that regards. You will be making very good money. What's your answer to our job offer?

REMBERT It's ironic isn't it? The first job offer was that I would be under you. Now it's that I would be over you with still higher pay.

Let's take matters in order, Dad. Please don't be in such a hurry for an answer. You used to be fond of lecturing me about priorities. May I suggest your first priority is to look at the violin?

RUDOLPH Okay, point well-made, Son. Let me play it so I can hear the sound.

[Rudolph plays a short passage of the Chaconne.]

Unbelievable! Yes, this is indeed a red Stradivarius. It even has the Stradivarius date of 1720 inside.

[Rudolph turns the violin over several times, looking at it intently.]

What a great find! You know, of course, how rare this violin is. What a coincidence it is that you of all people should be sitting at this same café when someone, you say a gypsy, started playing a Stradivarius. Raimund wouldn't have known the difference. By the way, how did you know it was a gypsy?

REMBERT   Dad, I didn't know for sure he was a gypsy. He just looked like one.

RUDOLPH   Okay, he may have been my friend Fritz Kreisler in disguise. Profiling can be unprofitable. But now, come on back with me to Cincinnati. My confirmation that your find is indeed a red Stradivarius will reassure our CEO Howard further. He will have no doubts about you, even though you didn't stay at Princeton as he and I once insisted you do.

REMBERT Thanks again, Dad. I liked working for Mr. Hill very much and would enjoy working with him again. When I worked for him last year in England, he always respected me. He encouraged me to make my own decisions. I would like to take the violin back home while I think about my two job offers.

RUDOLPH Another idea occurred to the Board and was approved. We suggest selling the violin to Herr Hamma. We bet we can make a quick profit. I will call him and see if he can join us quickly. We need to pay for our trip back home, and have change left over to buy beer. I'm joking, of course about needing change to buy beer.

No, really, by offering the violin to Herr Hamma at a very reasonable price, we can consolidate our relations with him. He is a very important Wurlitzer colleague. We must consolidate our relations with Mr. Hamma more so than with Mr. Hill who is not in Germany and who is more of an international competitor. So, with your permission, we'll invite him to join us at this beer garden and offer the violin to him for a very fair price.

REMBERT Dad, that sounds like bribery, but you always have a good sense of humor and feel for business, especially when it means selling my violin that I want to keep and take home.

Do you ever take into consideration what I want?

RUDOLPH   Relax son. What I am proposing would be best for you.

REMBERT   You mean, "What's good for you and the Wurlitzer Company."

Have some beer before business, right? And we will have beer with Mr. Hamma, right? But can we just walk away from this violin?

As an aside, how can a work of art as beautiful as this violin not have a provenance? It is like a lost Michelangelo sculpture in wood. It is a thing of beauty that has touched my soul. I don't want to sell it for your good or the good of Wurlitzer. Maybe, I'll take the Hill job offer. Mr. Hill listens to me.

[Rembert nods his head slowly.]

RUDOLPH   When conducting business, drinking beer is smart. Beer loosens tongues and tension. Besides, you should be suspicious of anyone who says no when offered a free beer. Reliable people don't drink fruit juice. Mr. Hamma loves beer and he is reliable. Would you like a free beer?

REMBERT   A free beer? Dad, you're conning me. There would be no free beer from you. You are insisting

I sell the violin.

RUDOLPH I am amused and pleased to hear you waxing about a violin you just found. I promise you there will be many other Stradivari in your life. Maybe, there will be many other beers and women too.

REMBERT Yes, I agree. Teetotalers are a threat to world peace and good violin businesses. We must always be suspicious of teetotalers and maybe Greeks offering free beer. And I should always do what you ask me to do, right?

After further thought and because I love you, you have my permission to sell my violin. Although allegedly I would be your boss as Head of Acquisitions, I'll defer to you. I'll make a personal sacrifice. So we'll do what you want with my violin. I am really angry, though, that you won't let me keep it. After all, it's mine; I used my own money to buy it. You are still my dad who is extorting me now to do what you want and what's good for Wurlitzer.

You are testing my loyalty. Yes, I'll have a beer, so you don't become suspicious of me. I'll drink beer every day from now on in order to be reliable in your eyes. I won't accept Mr. Hill's offer. But at least allow me to keep any profits I make selling my violin at your command to

Mr. Hamma.

RUDOLPH Of course, keep the profits. Just don't take what I am asking you to do personally. It's just business.

REMBERT Really? Is it really just business? A big deal makes a large personal sacrifice acceptable, right? Money means everything, right?

RUDOLPH Don't be a spoiled brat. You have a great job offer to head acquisitions, and you'll get more money than we first offered. We are truly trying eagerly to please you.

REMBERT We shall see. I don't recall my salary was ever discussed.

[Another lapse occurs as the lights are dimmed again and three more days pass.

The Chaconne is again played.]

SCENE #4

The sign outside the café has changed once more, and says simply, almost poetically, rhyming in German, "*Zwei Tage später trinken Wir wieder Bier*" and underneath this is a sign that is not the least bit poetic, "Two Days Later We Drink Beer Again." The year is still 1926.

Herr Hamma is wearing lederhosen and has a pot belly. He is also wearing a funny Bavarian hat with a feather sticking out of it.

(Actually, Herr Hamma is not a Bavarian caricature who wears lederhosen and a funny Bavarian hat. He speaks Hochdeutsch and is from Stuttgart. Obviously, he's then rather formal and stilted. <u>It's up to the director</u>, not the author, whether or not to dress Herr Hamma in either a pin-striped suit, lederhosen, or some other attire. The author doesn't care. Mr. Hamma who is dead might have cared though.)

RUDOLPH Herr Hamma, thank you for coming down so quickly to Berlin from Stuttgart. We have found a red Stradivarius of 1720. We thought you might be interested in purchasing it. My son and I have, of course, authenticated it, although we are concerned that there is no provenance.

HERR HAMMA Prost!

[As he lifts a stein of beer]

It's a real pleasure to be with your son and you. I dropped everything to be with you two. I was excited to hear you might sell a red Stradivarius

	to me. Seriously, the lack of provenance is a concern. But go on, please.
RUDOLPH	Prost.
	[As Rudolph lifts a stein of beer in return to Herr Hamma, Rembert lifts his stein too at the same time.]
	Our initial research here in Berlin suggests this is the red violin *The Mendelssohn*s owned over a hundred years ago. But. we have no proof, only a suspicion. The hundred-year gap in provenance is admittedly suspicious. Who owned the violin is a mystery. I agree with my son that the craftsmanship and the sound are those of a fine Stradivarius. We have no doubt. It is in excellent condition, and the tone is superb. Antonio was at his greatest around 1720.
HERR HAMMA	How much do you want and will you take Marks?
RUDOLPH	No Marks, please. We will sell it to you for $3,500. That's a more than a fair price.
	[Hamma picks up the violin, examines it for about 20 seconds shaking his head up and down, and then starts playing the Chaconne. After all, there is no repetitiveness in playing the Chaconne each time there is a pause in

this play, because every great violinist, every great violin dealer, and every great theater attendee surely knows and loves Bach's Chaconne.]

HERR HAMMA What a beautiful tone! Okay, I'll pay you $3,000. I know that's less, but I can't stop myself from bargaining. I've bargained all my life. Perhaps, I can return your kindness someday if you accept. I trust your authentications, and I also agree it is a true Stradivarius. I can pay cash, write a check on an American account, or arrange a bank draft.

Rembert, what do you think?

REMBERT I definitely agree it is a Stradivarius. The tone and craftsmanship are uniquely that of Stradivarius, and the Stradivari label is intact. The tone is breathtaking. The red color is beautiful. This is an absolutely superb, red Stradivarius of 1720 when the master was near his peak in his "golden period." It's really a treasure.

HAMMA By the way, thank you for selling this violin to me at such a bargain price.

RUDOLPH Done. A bank draft will be fine, and we accept your $3,000 offer. I'll give you a receipt of money and proof of sale right now. We are selling the violin to you, because we need to pay our way back home to Cincinnati.

[Rudolph writes out a receipt.]

You can take the violin with you.

HERR HAMMA Prost,…

[As he lifts his stein of beer confirming the deal]

…*und zum unser Bruderhaft*! Prost, and to our brotherhood. It will be a bank draft that I will get for you before you leave. I can do this here in Berlin tomorrow. When do you leave?

RUDOLPH Rembert and I leave tomorrow, late afternoon. We must get back home

HERR HAMMA Great! I'll take the bank draft to the Hotel Adlon Kempinski. That's where you are staying? By the way, did you come to Berlin just to sell me this violin?

RUDOLPH Yes, we're at the Adlon Kempinski, and no, I came primarily to make sure Rembert accepts a job offer we have made him that he's now accepted. He has proven his faith in Wurlitzer to me. We'll see you later tomorrow morning.

HERR HAMMA It's been a pleasure.

[He lifts his stein of beer again, Rudolph and Rembert reciprocate by lifting their steins of beer. The deal is consummated by lifting beer

to each other. It's good business drinking beer between reliable business associates.

Herr Hamma gets up, extends his right hand to shake hands with Rembert and Rudolph, and then departs.

A short time later after Herr Hamma has departed]

REMBERT Dad, I hope you appreciate the sacrifice I just made selling that violin. I will miss it very much. I played it every evening over the last two weeks, and then I dreamed of playing it. I even took it into the bathroom with me playing it on the can. It's a glorious instrument. It became part of my soul, even my body. By God, I will buy it back from Herr Hamma if he ever sells it. That violin has become part of me. I love that violin. I loved playing it. I must possess it again. Most importantly, I trust I have proven my faith in Wurlitzer by having agreed to sell what was mine and even part of my soul. I don't believe I am getting any Faustian bargain agreeing to work for Wurlitzer and with you.

RUDOLPH You are getting a bargain. What you do not understand is that you need to separate from your violin. You need to grow up. For your own mental health, the violin and you need to separate.

REMBERT *[Calmy and reflectively]*

Ah, it just occurred to me possibly you are right. Possessing the violin might be a form of an Oedipus Complex where unconsciously, this violin I love represents my mother. I must possess the violin that is my mother again and again in order to displace you. I must possess and then sell more Stradivari violins. I will become a serial possessor of rare violins. Am I just being facetious or stupidly pedantic, like Freud?

Freud was right. So are you. There is an Oedipal connection to my love of my red violin. I loved my mother very much. I remember now how much it disturbed me as a youngster when you kissed her. I wanted to possess her. I was jealous of you. I never got over that jealousy.

RUDOLPH I know Freud would agree with you. I'm pleased with your flash of sophomoric insight. You are not being facetious. I didn't have to explain to you what I had already understood. You will see the red violin again, I am sure. You will also see your mother again, I assure you. And you will see and fondle many, many beautiful instruments again and again. And you will have grown up psychologically.

Herr Hamma promised he would reciprocate

our kindness at some future time, and he is a man of honor. It's time, anyway, for you to recover from your Oedipal Complex and understand your psychological needs better. It's time for you to be a man. You don't have to be with your mother and the red violin every day. Have no doubt, there will be many, many violins in your future working with Wurlitzer. Hopefully, there will not be many, many women.

REMBERT That red violin is a mystery violin. It's in my soul. It's in my unconscious. It is a conflict for me to let it go, as it would be to let my mother go. Selling it is like selling part of my soul or even my mother. I feel no Faustian bargain in return working for Wurlitzer allegedly over you at a high salary. I feel no fulfillment without possessing it. But now I understand better why my life's mission will be to possess and control as many Stradivari and rare instruments as possible. My soul demands this commitment.

RUDOLPH Relax, son. You'll recover. You're overexplaining your understanding. You're intellectualizing. You sound like a tragic Shakespearean character like Othello and Macbeth who always talked too much. Time will give you other answers. Rather than dreaming of possessing your mother, now you can dream of possessing more violins, as rare as your mother. It's all right, son. You will recover and not have the same dreams. It's even okay to intellectualize sometimes, especially over alcohol.

REMBERT You are as tiresome as I am at amateur psychoanalysis. Enough! But I do want to say I am really frosted. I find a rare Stradivari violin. I buy it with my money. I fall in love with it. You demand I sell it to Herr Hamma as a test of my loyalty. You make a better job offer, because I found a rare violin, to be head of acquisitions. Then you expected me to turn down a job offer with Mr. Hill, a man I like very much. And I've insulted him by selling a Stradivari to Herr Hamma rather than to him. I just wonder what else you will expect of me. Will you expect me to sell my soul to you again?

RUDOLPH No, Faust sold his soul only once. We expect you to accept our job offer to be head of acquisitions, to work with many rare Stradivari, and to receive a very handsome salary while being with your family. We expect you to be a mature, rational businessman who drinks beer and who will maintain relations with our German colleagues and relatives in the music business.

REMBERT I accept.

RUDOLPH That was tough.

SCENE #5

There has been a time-lapse of 30 years, and Rembert is back at the Berlin beer garden again, this time with Herr Hamma. Time has flown by so quickly that the café is still the same. Red lights, as if one were in a bordello, flash on and off announcing the opportunity for Rembert to buy the red violin he loves so much. The red color reminds him of illicit sex, and he suddenly remembers his morther again who has died. Repressed thoughts flood his mind uncontrollably. The year is 1956, and a sign outside says, "*Wir feiern 1956 mit Bier und eine feine rote Geige*," and underneath, "We celebrate 1956 with beer and a fine red violin."

HERR HAMMA Rembert, thank you for coming with your busy schedule back to Germany so quickly at my request. Your company is well known to all of us now in the violin business. You have accomplished a great deal. How many Stradivari violins have you purchased since I last saw you in 1926?

REMBERT My Company has purchased, handled, or possessed on consignment over a hundred Stradivari violins since then. Almost all were on consignment. I am doing well. How are you doing?

HERR HAMMA That is an astounding number of Stradivari violins to have possessed. No one ever before can cite a number like that for handling and selling Stradivari violins. Casanova may not have possessed even that number of women. Your record is most remarkable. Not even Luigi Tarisio or Baron Knoop possessed as many Stradivari violins as you have. Most musicians don't believe that you have had so many great violins. They would believe you more if you claimed you had had sex with a hundred women or even with your mother.

REMBERT Thank you so much, I suppose. I was not really a collector; I was a dealer. Most of the instruments I handled were on consignment. When I possessed them on consignment, it was like casual sex with no permanency. One friend even told me I was a rare violin pimp.

Others, sometimes, gave me credit for owning instruments I didn't own. But I did just buy *La Pucelle* last year. Sometimes, I did buy fiddles.

Your English now is very good. If people don't believe what I have done, that is their problem. It's not my problem.

HERR HAMMA Yes, for business I had to learn good English. Thank God I was not in East Berlin. The Russians are terrible. My city, Stuttgart, was heavily bombed, but not as bad as Dresden, thank God. Unfortunately, I must tell you we have gone through hell in this last war. We are still very much feeling the consequences. We

	have not fully recovered. Many of my friends and relatives died. I was fortunate to have survived. My workshop in Stuttgart was destroyed. Businesses are still slowly recovering. The Marshall Plan has helped.
REMBERT	My father and I were always very fond of you. You helped us with many business deals. We sincerely wish the best for you and your family, and, of course, Germany.
HERR HAMMA	Thank you. Sadly, I need money now, and I want to sell the red violin to the man who authenticated it and sold it to me. You and your father were exceedingly kind to me. I feel a moral obligation to respond – if we agree on price. So, I am giving you a right of first refusal. You can buy the red violin for a very reasonable price of $20,000.
REMBERT	Herr Hamma, when you called me in New York and told me you wanted to sell *The Mendelssohn*, I was thrilled. I dropped everything to fly to West Berlin. Someday, we hope The Wall will come down. It's been a difficult time with East Germany being under the Russians and separate from West Germany. We can't even see or call our relatives in Schöneck, East Germany. We have lost contact with relatives we love. Fortunately, we can still see our relatives in Vienna.

HERR HAMMA   Yes, it has been very difficult.

REMBERT   You are still a man who gets directly to the point and says without hesitation what he has on his mind. Thanks, too, for your sentiments. I am glad you are well, and I respect your directness and situation. In no way do I want to take advantage of you.

Yes, many of our relatives in Germany died during the war. The war was a tragic time for so many of those whose ancestry is German. We are blessed to be Americans who have more than enough money to put beer and food on the table. Maybe someday, The Wall will come down, and we can see our relatives again in East Germany.

HERR HAMMA   *Gott sei Dank.* Thanks be to God.

REMBERT   *[Again, related calmly]*

Yes, God be thanked. I have always had a special fondness for the red violin that we now call *The Mendelssohn*. It is a magical violin. It is still a violin of mystery. It is a violin that I have dreamed about repeatedly for many years. I even had wet dreams thinking of it at night after I first found it almost 30 years ago. Who owned it over the hundred-year provenance gap, we still don't know definitely. *The Mendelssohn*s and the great violinist Joseph

Joachim may have owned it. We're not sure. It took years to research the provenance even while you were the owner. We didn't list it in the Wurlitzer inventory as *The Mendelssohn* originally after I found it in Berlin in the late 1920's, because we were not positive *The Mendelssohn*s owned it. In fact, we didn't list it at all, because the violin was mine, personally. When I discovered it, I wasn't working for Wurlitzer. There's really no documentation. I found it and sold it to you, and when I buy it from you, there will be no business documentation, because it will be my private, personal treasure. Owning it will permit me, if I want, a psychological relapse to what it meant originally.

How do we find documentation that doesn't exist? I don't know for sure if *The Mendelssohn*s owned the violin. I really don't care. When there is love, there need be no documentation.

I agree to the price of $20,000. There will be no bargaining. I'll send you a bank draft. I just want to possess the violin and its beauty. In my mind, there must be no more *coitus interruptus*. I have felt a void in my soul for many years after being forced to sell the violin, my violin, to you in 1926. I will never sell it again. I am mentally exhausted dreaming of it. My father

	wanted me to grow up accepting a separation from it. I am afraid I never did.
HERR HAMMA	For years, I knew you were conflicted, because of your constant questioning about the violin when we talked about other matters. It was obvious to me you missed it deeply. No bargaining? I'm a bit disappointed you didn't, although I was quite sure you wouldn't bargain. Owning it was an idée fixe for you.

By the way, your German is still very good. I will give you a handwritten receipt. Send me a bank draft later, and you can take the red violin now. *Auf Wiedersehen.* |
| **REMBERT** | Herr Hamma, please don't be in such a hurry to leave. Let's go out to dinner to celebrate. We have so much to be thankful for now. |
| **HERR HAMMA** | No, I have to go, and thanks for coming so quickly to Berlin. I have always enjoyed this beer garden since it was here that I bought the red violin from your Dad and you. |
| **REMBERT** | My soul is at peace again.

Be assured you will receive a bank draft soon. Then, send me a receipt. I will never sell my red Stradivarius. It is part of my psyche. I feel complete. I doubt I will even tell my family about how important the violin is to me |

	spiritually. There would be too much to explain. They wouldn't understand. My id is now satisfied.
HERR HAMMA	There's no problem. Take the violin. I have no concerns about you sending a bank draft to me in Stuttgart. I'll give you a handwritten receipt right now.
	[Hamma writes out a receipt while talking.]
	Unfortunately, I have to catch the next train soon to Stuttgart and home. *Bis bald sehen.* I'll see you soon again, I hope, and I await your bank draft. *Gott sei Dank.*
REMBERT	*Gott sei Dank.* Thanks be to God. *Auf Wiedersehen.*

SCENE #6

It is now 1957 in Rembert's office in New York, a year after Rembert bought *The Mendelssohn* from Herr Hamma. He is talking with Francesco Mendelssohn, the grand nephew of Felix Mendelssohn.

FRANCESCO   Hello, Rembert. What a pleasure it is to see you again.

REMBERT   Yes, it has been several years since I learned that you had owned *The Mendelssohn* in 1913. But now that I own the fiddle again after having bought it from Herr Hamma in 1956, I still don't understand what happened between 1913 and 1926 when I found the fiddle after you had lost it. A gypsy was playing it back then in 1926 when I was at an outdoor Berlin beer restaurant.

FRANCESCO   It's a long story. Briefly, I've always had a problem with drinking. I have been such a clod. You may recall that one time in 1950 after a concert, I returned home on East 62nd Street absolutely stewed. I couldn't even enter my home. Then, in an alcoholic daze, I realized I was at the wrong house. I dumped my famous *Piatti Stradivarius Cello* on the ground, and found my house. I forgot about my cello.

REMBERT   That's not funny. Well, actually it is funny.

FRANCESCO I was so used to leaving my Stradivarius at bars to pay my drinking bills, I thought I had just left my fiddle at a bar where I had been earlier after the concert. The next morning, my housekeeper asked me if a cello she had found on the street was mine. She said the trash people were about to pick it up, but she had grabbed it quickly.

REMBERT What has that to do with *The Mendelssohn?*

FRANCESCO Well, you may recall, because a book has been written about my cello and me, about the time I escaped from Nazi Germany on my bicycle going to Switzerland carrying my cello. If I had had *The Mendelssohn*, I would have taken it. It was more valuable than the *Piatti*. But I had lost *The Mendelssohn.*

REMBERT You lost *The Mendelssohn*?

FRANCESCO Yes, later in 1913 after I bought *The Mendelssohn* from a Mr. Hammig, I was really learning how to drink. Mr. Hammig was not the Mr. Hamma you know from whom you bought the red violin. After a concert and being thoroughly smashed, I left the fiddle on the sidewalk. Just as I would leave *The Piatti* in bars to ensure payment, I left it on the street to ensure payment to the trash collector. The next morning, the trash collector picked it up. He was pissed at me, because I had not paid for his services for weeks. He called me a Jewish sod. In those days in Berlin, one paid directly for trash services. So, he may have sold it to the gypsy you heard playing it or he may have sold it to someone else. I heard rumors it somehow ended up in China for a while.

REMBERT You couldn't make up a story like that. Truth can be stranger than fiction. Unbelievable! I remember the time you took a cello I made in Mirecourt rather than *The Piatti* on a trip. Then in a drunken stupor while smoking, you set the house on fire where you were staying. My cello burned up, but *The Piatti* was saved.

Truth is better than fiction. Sometimes, fiction is truth. You're entertaining, but dangerous to the health of musical instruments. It's fortunate I found *The Mendelssohn* in 1926. If you had kept it, you probably would have set it on fire or left it at a bar. Fortunately, you just lost it to a trash collector.

FRANCESCO I'm grateful. You are true and dear to my drunken heart.

You Rembert are "The Resurrector of *The Mendelssohn*." I loved *The Mendelssohn*. It was part of my soul. When I lost it, I lost part of my soul. Alcohol helped me forget.

REMBERT Now I own it and it is part of my soul too. It is in both our souls.

How do we justify our existence? I ask this because you have abandoned your greatness and the greatness of your great Uncle Felix by becoming an alcoholic? Why?

FRANCESCO What a great question! I am Jewish. I am a world-class cellist. Musical halls beg for my performances as a virtuoso cellist. Felix, a musical genius, was Jewish. Polite people begged him to give personal performances. Yet, we are discarded. We are seen as inferiors. Because we are Jewish we are not accepted.

REMBERT There are always injustices. My father told me long ago not to take disturbing matters personally. When I challenged him that selling my beloved red violin to Hamma was an effrontery to my soul, he told me his request was just business. When I was made to sell it, I lost part of my soul. At least when Faust sold his soul to the devil, he got a violin. Maybe, it was our red violin.

FRANCESCO You and I are not very different. I am not referring to the fact that I am Jewish and you are an Aryan German American. That difference matters to society, but not to us.

REMBERT What do you mean?

FRANCESCO I mean you were mentally disturbed for years after your father made you sell our red violin. There was an incompleteness in your soul. I, on the other hand, have felt gaps in my soul by not being accepted by polite society as truly a great musician, because I am Jewish. As a result, there has been incompleteness in my soul.

REMBERT I was a business man out of necessity. You chose to find relief by becoming an alcoholic world-class musician. How strange that it is that we see each other as being alike! Both of us sought to recover our souls.

FRANCESCO I admire you for having resurrected my ancestry. Yes, I feel you resurrected not just *The Mendelssohn*, but also my Jewish ancestry. You have preserved my inheritance. My alcoholism is for me an amusing fraud. Others now forgive me for being Jewish, because I am an alcoholic.

REMBERT Several times over the years, you told me you sought beauty even while being an alcoholic. What did you mean?

FRANCESCO I feel like a poet being asked to explain a particular poem. I've sought beauty all my life. When I played my Stradivari cello, I possessed beauty.

REMBERT How do you define beauty?

REMBERT How do we define beauty? How do we define love? I do know that all Stradivari instruments are works of art, but not all are works of beauty. Some are comparable to the Michelangelo *Pietà*, to the *Last Supper* by da Vinci, or to the *Alba Madonna* by Raphael. Like the Chaconne, that has a beauty of musical structure, the best Stradivari violins are incomparable sculptures in wood that can produce glorious, breathtaking sounds. That is a musical synthesis. The ultimate mystery of how that can be leaves me bewildered with wonder. How is that synthesis possible? Even today, why Stradivari instruments can have such beautiful sounds remains a mystery. Is it the "f" stops or mineralization? We don't really know. We still guess. It is a mystery how beautiful sounds can come from wood. Beauty is a mystery. Surely, God favored man with the beauty of red Stradivarius violins or cellos like my *Piatti* with particularly beautiful sounds. When I hear Yehudi Menuhin play the Chaconne on his Strad violin or Yo-Yo Ma on his Strad cello, I feel the way they play mirrors how I feel inside. That is beauty. I try to play the same way with beauty. In heaven, God ordains that his angels play the Chaconne only with red Stradivari like mine. Did you know that? That is true beauty.

SCENE #7

More time has now passed, and it is now 1963, just seven years after 1956 when Rembert bought the red violin. The Chaconne is played again softly and slowly as if for a funeral dirge. Red lights are dimmed briefly. Rembert just died, and his wife Lee is in mourning, softly crying. She is in the office (essentially, the office in Scene #1 and #6) talking to a reporter. A sign on the wall says, "*Wir feiern nicht das Jahre 1963, das Jahr, in dem mein Mann starb.*" Underneath the sign in German, there is the English translation, "We do not celebrate this year when my husband died." Above this signage is a plaque saying, "Rembert Wurlitzer Co." and below it, "New York."

REPORTER for MUSIC TIMES

Thank you for meeting with me, Mrs. Wurlitzer. Your husband was a great man. He is sorely missed in the rare musical instrument world. There has seldom been anyone like him who dealt with so many rare instruments and who had the integrity he had when authenticating. I understand he or a Wurlitzer handled, repaired, authenticated and/or sold as a dealer about 158 Stradivari violins. Of course, he sold on consignment many other rare musical instruments than just Strads.

LEE

Yes, my husband was a marvel. He was kind, unusually bright, and extremely knowledgeable and intuitive about rare musical instruments, especially Strads. His memory was fantastic, and he could recount particulars about hundreds and hundreds of rare violins and thousands of musical instruments. His personal knowledge about rare musical instruments was encyclopedic.

REPORTER But how many Stradivari violins did he possess? Frankly, reports that he handled and then sold maybe 158 Stradivari violins seem preposterous. Musicians I talk to don't believe the figures. Two musicians told me the 158 figure is ridiculous.

LEE My Rembert was one of the world's greatest dealers ever of rare violins. He thought in terms of possessing them, if even only briefly, through consignment, rarely through purchase. As you mentioned, Rembert, together with his father, dealt with at least 158 Stradivari violins. Other Stradivaris were handled at the Wurlitzer Music Company where Rembert and his father Rudolph had dealt with rare violins. The total number of Strads handled by a Wurlitzer was greater than 158. Many of these violins were handled on consignment. Some though were purchased by Wurlitzer, held sometimes for months or years, and then sold. I've never seen a serial human relationship greater in number than the number of serial relationships my Rembert had with violins.

REPORTER   What did Mr. Goodkind think about the huge numbers of Stradivari violins Rembert handled?

LEE   Mr. Goodkind was fascinated with the numbers of violins Rembert had possessed. He facetiously referred to Rembert as the "Casanova of violins." Brief possession of violins was a fixation for Rembert. At the same time, he was never a womanizer, thank God. You might say Rembert was a "violinizer."

REPORTER   Wow! I've never heard anyone before refer to Rembert as the "Casanova of violins," or as a violinizer. The psychiatric implications are diverting.

LEE   My remarks are not to be quoted. Although the records do not show, while Rembert was head of purchases for Wurlitzer, whether it was Rudolph or Rembert who bought or dealt with a particular rare violin, the numbers cumulatively were impressive.

REPORTER   How did you keep track?

LEE   We kept "Black Books" for violins we authenticated or dealt with peripherally. Our inventories were separately recorded on stock cards.

REPORTER   What about other great collectors? Were there

LEE   any who matched your husband in the number of Stradivari violins handled?

LEE   Essentially, Rembert was primarily a dealer. He really didn't collect violins. Most of the violins he handled were on consignment. Out of personal interest in answering your question, I did some recent research. Even Luigi Tarisio, a great collector and dealer, had just twenty-four Stradivari violins, and Alessandro Cozio Di Salabue, known as a supreme collector and dealer, had only ten. Baron Knoop had about the same number. Admittedly, my husband did not own all the Stradivari violins he handled at the same time, but, as a authenticator, restorer, dealer, and seller, he was among a rare breed. There have been other dealers who may have handled as many or more violins than he, so let's not put too much importance on his numbers. Fernando Sacconi did most of our restoration work.

REPORTER   Your allusions to Rembert as the "Casanova of violins" or as a "violinizer" are provocative.

LEE   Many find Rembert's history of love for violins fascinating. Dr. Freud suggested to him once there were profound sexual connections. He even told Rembert his fascination for *The Mendelssohn* could be explained as an Oedipal Complex. Rembert agreed with that analysis. His love for *The Mendelssohn* that he had found was like his love for his mother. He hid this illicit love by not listing *The Mendelssohn* in his inventory. But I knew. The inventory was meant for instruments on sale.

The real reason he did not list *The Mendelssohn* in his inventory was that for him it was a "keeper."

REPORTER Did Rembert actually collect anything?

LEE I would say he was a collector of pochettes, a few odd instruments such as a Quinton and bows, or other instruments with defects that were not particularly saleable. *The Mendelssohn* was not part of any collection. Rembert saw *The Mendelssohn* as part of himself and as much as his hand was part of his body. His psychological connections to that fiddle were profound.

REPORTER Did Rembert ever lie to you or to others?

LEE Not to my knowledge. Like any human, he made mistakes. They weren't lies. He was a man of great integrity.

REPORTER What about records from other dealers?

LEE Luigi Tarisio kept no records of any of his transactions, nor inventory of his collections. That is another reason why the Tarisio database is compromised. An estimated up to 1,100 instruments were made by Antonio Stradivari. Many Stradivaris are simply unaccounted for now, although they are known historically. More than a few owners hid or still deny ownership. Many Stradivaris were lost or damaged irreparably. There will probably never be a complete list of Stradivari instruments.

REPORTER Does your company still retain the famous *Mendelssohn?*

LEE Yes, I still have that violin. But it is hidden. It was a secret possession that I can divulge to you now that Rembert is dead. I couldn't even tell my daughter or son about the violin, because it would have been like divulging an affair. It was an affair.

Rembert wouldn't even talk about the red violin with his children either. There was just too much emotional overlay that he would find uncomfortable divulging to them. I had the same problem.

REPORTER What did the well-known Francesco von *Mendelssohn* say?

LEE Francesco von *Mendelssohn*, who lived in New York, was a descendent of *The Mendelssohn*s, He became a very good friend of ours, because

Rembert had "resurrected" *The Mendelssohn*. Francesco admitted sheepishly he had left the violin in a drunken stupor on a sidewalk in 1913. Trash collectors picked it up.

REPORTER Are you saying one can love a violin?

LEE Yes, indeed. There is no doubt that is true. Just ask famous violinists who play famous "Strads" if they love their violin. For that matter, ask violists who play famous violas if they love their instruments. One might even say that a rare Strad can possess its owner. Rembert used to say he possessed *The Mendelssohn*, but sometimes I thought it possessed him. I am not sure he actually loved *The Mendelssohn* any more than Casanova loved his conquests. But have no doubt possessing his red violin kept his psychological needs for love and achievement at bay.

REPORTER Is it unusual for a rare violin to disappear like *The Mendelssohn* did for decades?

LEE Stradivari violins disappear. Many that are historically known are not known now. Some emerged later out of hiding like *The Sleeping Beauty* of 1704 that lay hidden within castle walls for generations. Rembert resurrected *The Mendelssohn* that had been missing. I've known wives who disappeared from their husbands for years. Why should rare violins be any different?

Disappearance can be a survival technique for stolen violins and adulterous women. Disappearance can even work well for unruly husbands who fear their wives might kill them.

REPORTER What are you going to do with Rembert's company?

LEE It's my company now, thank you. Now that my husband has died, I have taken over the company. I can say proudly that our company bought, sold, authenticated and/or restored more than half the world's six-hundred known Stradivari. Not all Strads were violins. We have supplied instruments to Fritz Kreisler, David Oistrakh, and Isaac Stern, among others. My company has a remarkable history. It would sell for a premium price, just based on the value of the brand name. "Wurlitzer" means music to millions of people. Nonetheless, I do not want to sell the company and its brand name. I do not want anyone to use ever again the name of my beloved Rembert Wurlitzer.

REPORTER Do you have a buyer in mind?

LEE Yes, and it may surprise you, that information is not confidential now. It's already been leaked throughout the music world. There is a music company named Moennig in Philadelphia. I am negotiating with them to buy our inventory of important, old, rare musical instruments. They would use their name, not the name of Rembert Wurlitzer in selling that inventory to musicians, not primarily to collectors.

REPORTER What's in the inventory?

LEE There are at least 1,400 objects including Guadagninis, Amatis, del Gesùs, Gaglianos, Roccas, Bergonzis, Stainers, Lorenzinis, Guarneris, and Giuseppes. Not all are on consignment.

REPORTER What might the Wurlitzer collection be worth?

LEE *[Lee laughs.]*

"Who knows? Until an old instrument actually changes hands, its value is unpredictable, especially in the present inflationary situation." I'm not really that interested in getting the maximum amount possible or feasible. I want to sell our inventory at a reasonable price to a company like Moennig that would intend to sell the inventory to musicians. Selling to musicians may be, in fact, a condition for purchase in many cases where there are no consignment constraints.

REPORTER So many Stradivari violins have odd names. Can you explain?

LEE Many of the great Stradivari violins have engaging nicknames like *The Messiah, The Dolphin, The Virgin, The Lady Blunt, The Contessa, The Venus, The Sleeping Beauty*, and *The Molitor*, owned by Bonaparte. Nicknames have added to the magical allure of these magnificent instruments. A nickname gives a "halo of mystery" and a hint to provenance. It's a bit like provocative "Haloes of Mystery" given to famous women like "*The Daughter of a Whore*" for Elizabeth I; "*The Suffragist*" for Susan Anthony; "*Harriet, the Sl*ave," for Harriet Tubman; or "*The Notorious RGB*" for Ruth Ginsberg. Rembert thought of rare violins as beautiful, interesting women. He enjoyed possessing them briefly.

REPORTER What about stories behind the great Stradivari violins? They are almost legendary.

LEE Some Stradivari violins have amazing stories of being lost at sea like the *Red Diamond* of 1732 or the *Hartley* that went down with the Titanic and was later recovered. Others, like the *Sleeping Be*auty of 1704 or *The Mendelssohn* of 1720, were resurrected after many years. Stradivaris are often indeed instruments of mystery and legend.

REPORTER What won't you do?

LEE "I would never sell them at retail or auction

them off, since that would mean that the collection, which has been insured for more than a decade at $1 million and includes some 1,400 "objects," would be gobbled up by collectors. I wouldn't want to see that. I want the instruments to be used by musicians." Rembert was a good violinist. He wasn't really a collector. He didn't want to keep Stradivari instruments out of the hands of musicians. His father, Rudolph, had studied to be a concert violinist. Musicians were important to Rembert and me, especially excellent ones without sufficient money to buy a beautiful, rare instrument. A music company like Moennig would sell inventory to musicians, not collectors. That would be contractual. Maximizing what we might get would not be our prime incentive. I may even give a viola to my daughter Marianne who is a violist. I would definitely consider giving some instruments to excellent musicians who are not wealthy or even to charity.

REPORTER Are you talking about the social issue of haves and have nots?

LEE Yes, I am. We have an obligation to help others. That is not socialism. We felt an obligation to help musicians who could not afford to buy a rare musical instrument.

REPORTER What is the most valuable violin you own?

LEE Perhaps the most valuable now on hand is the *Hellier* Strad, which was commissioned from Stradivari by an English family named Hellier. It has had only three owners. It might be worth as much as $300,000. I may give this violin to a charity.

REPORTER Don't you have a son named Rudy? Isn't he interested in the family business?

LEE He is a well-known writer. He's written screenplays and quite a few books. He's not interested in running the business.

REPORTER There are so many in your family named Rudy. How do you keep them apart?

LEE It's difficult.

REPORTER Okay, I will limit my further questioning, although surely you would like to say more in honor of your husband. I sincerely do not want to push you.

What do you feel when a Stradivarius is played?

LEE When one hears the Chaconne played well,

[The Chaconne is softly playing again in the background.]

...my heart trembles. When I hear the

Chaconne played well on a Stradivarius whether a cello, viola, or violin, my heart throbs. It is an emotional experience for me when I hear a dazzling Stradivarius beautifully playing gorgeous music. There may be no greater beauty than hearing Bach's Chaconne played beautifully on a beautiful red Stradivarius. For me, it is emotional. It is like deep love in its intensity. Experiencing this beauty is, well, excuse me, it's like beautiful sex.

Rembert and his father, Rudolph Henry, who studied to be a concert violinist, used to say possessing and then playing a rare, beautiful violin with gorgeous tones was like possessing and having sex with a beautiful woman. Rembert used to call me sometimes, "my lovely violin." Sex with him was great.

REPORTER Aren't there other Stradivari made by relatives of Antonio?

LEE Yes, indeed there are other Stradivari. Antonio's sons Omobono and Francesco made violins that are technically Stradivari violins, although their violins are not usually of the same quality as the violins their father made.

[The Chaconne is played again for a full 30 seconds. Lee listens intently and reflectively, and then smiles.]

REPORTER   You seem lost in thought.

LEE   Yes, I was remembering my husband and his wisdom. Stradivari violins now sell for a million or more, far more than what my husband ever paid.

Rembert was a masterpiece himself like his red violin.

There is a qualified, private buyer who is unusually interested. I cannot discuss details.

REPORTER   Is there any significance to the fact that *The Mendelssohn* is red?

LEE   Yes, the red color of *The Mendelssohn* is of significance. The red violin Rembert identified is not the only red Stradivarius known. The *Red Diamond* comes to my mind. Although most Stradivaris do not have a deep red color, those that do may have a more resonant sound than others not red. It may be because of a unique, red, mineral varnish that Antonio used from time-to-time, how the "f" stops were cut or even the density of wood that created a beautiful tone. But keep in mind we did not categorize Stradivari violins according to color or specifically the color red, and certainly not sound.

REPORTER   Does red have any other significance?

LEE The red color for a Strad can hold a special allure. Let me read you what the *Strad* wrote. I just happen to have a copy.

[There is another time warp since the Strad's September 2018 issue is being used. Lee pauses while putting on her glasses, and then reads.]

"The significance of red in our lives goes back to the Neanderthals, who buried their dead in red ochre. Every human culture has assigned some version of power to this color. In ancient China it was the color of health and prosperity. In the Arab world it signified divine favor and vitality. The Roman Empire was ruled by a class whose name, "coccinati," literally meant "those who wear red." It is the color of kings and queens, cardinals and demons."

Red is the color of illicit sex and Rembert saw sex in his red violin. That is partly why he never listed it in his inventory. Unconsciously he thought his love for violins was illicit, because his violin affairs were so brief. His affair with *The Mendelssohn* was not brief. It was licit.

Although there are many Stradivari, those that are red are often truly special and seen as sexy, like *The Mendelssohn* of 1720, *The Red Diamond* of 1732 or *The Sassoon* of 1733.

REPORTER Why do you want to sell? I've been afraid to ask that question. I really haven't wanted to offend you, and I apologize if I have.

LEE I'm tired. I'm ready to retire. I want to smell the roses. I want to go to the theater. I want to just look at the Moon and drink wine while hearing the Chaconne and thinking of Rembert. I want to read naughty novels like *Delta of Venus* and *Lady Chatterly's Lover* again.

REPORTER What's your most important memory?

LEE That's an interesting question. All memories fade or disappear over time, but at least during the rest of my life, my love for Rembert will not in the least bit diminish. We had a three-way lust affair: for each other and for a red Stradivari violin. One observer commented that three-way relationship seemed incestuous.

REPORTER Any final comments, please?

LEE I am proud to have loved and supported my husband. I cry, knowing he died from a heart attack at such an early age of fifty-nine. I miss him terribly.

[Lee starts to cry, pauses briefly, then continues speaking while sniffling.]

I will do my best to run the company well,

although we no longer have anyone with us that we can truly rely upon for authentications. We will liquidate over time. I certainly have no intentions of purchasing any instruments now. Neither my daughter nor my son wants to run the company. It's time for me to enjoy afternoon naps. I want to withdraw into my shell. Life has been good to me, giving me a fine daughter and son, and a wonderful husband. I'm not ready to die yet.

Thanks to God.t

[As the lights dim, they turn a deep red while Chopin's Funeral March is played slowly, preferably on a violin or two violins rather than a piano, as a dirge. A picture (seen below) of the deep red Stradivarius Mendelssohn *is shown on a screen. Francisco gives a brief eulogy. Then the dirge abruptly ends as Rembert's life abruptly ended with a heart attack.]*

FRANCESCO My dear friend has left us. He gave so much to the world by preserving beauty. The world has lost a treasure. He was a man of beauty. I'll miss him deeply. I am going to get a drink. [Francesco staggers off stage.]

Postscript

The Mendelssohn was bought in 1990 by Mr. Pitcairn who gave it to his daughter, the famous violinist, Elizabeth Pitcairn. She played her violin once, not that many years ago, in Sarasota, Florida, where the author and his wife, Ann, have a home.

Elizabeth Pitcairn is reported as saying she loves her violin and that it has given her life meaning by being her "most inspiring mentor and friend." Rembert might have made similar comments.

Records

Mr. Herbert Goodkind's book listing about 635 Stradivari violins is the most authoritative source listing Stradivari violins. Rembert's daughter Marianne helped Mr. Goodkind with his recordations and memos. Rembert's inventory was given to Charles Beare in England, who, in turn, gave access to Mr. David Fulton, a collector in Seattle. Charles Beare had worked with Wurlitzer. His son Freddie is a dealer in England.

This picture of the *Red Mendelssohn* can be shown on a screen as the lights finally dim in red, and then house lights are turned on.

Copies of the author's book, *Rembert,* can be made available at Intermission or afterwards, if a play is ever performed. All profits would go to the theater.

Intermezzo

At this point having presented the play that attempts to explain when the Red Violin was discovered, and moreover having presented evidence as to what violin was the Red Violin, I would like to address secondary issues.

Chapter 8

Are Strads Good Investments?

Stradivari violins now sell for many millions, far more than what Rembert paid. The highest price paid up to 2011 for a Stradivarius violin was the "*Lady Blunt*" Stradivarius of 1721, which sold for a record $16 million in 2011 to an anonymous buyer who loaned the violin to violinist Anne Akiko Meyers who is still alive. Earlier, in the 1890s, W.E. Hill & Sons had bought the violin for an undisclosed amount from Lady Ann Blunt and sold it to an important collector, but not to the Wurlitzer Company or Rembert.

David Fulton confirmed recently in private correspondence that Rembert had *La Pucelle* on consignment in 1953 from Mr. Frank Otwell. "Finally, on 5/11/55, Wurlitzers purchased the fiddle from consignment. It's interesting that Wurlitzer bought the fiddle for $25,000 while the consignment had been for $42,000." Mr. Otwell was apparently eager to sell the fiddle. When Mr. Fulton's foundation sold the fiddle in 2019, it fetched $22 million.[18] All should agree that was an impressive financial appreciation.

A rare viola made by Stradivari in 1719, The "MacDonald" Viola, purchased at one time by The Rudolph Wurlitzer

---

[18] Mr. Fulton gave me permission to relate this information.

Company[19] for less than a hundred thousand dollars did not sell at the reserve price of $45 million set by Sotheby's in 2014. It was the first to be on the market in fifty years, according to Sotheby's auction house. It is also one of only two Stradivari violas still privately owned. The other is held in the Library of Congress in Washington, DC.

Over time Strads and other rare musical instruments have been good investments. Over more than 150 years, rare musical instruments have appreciated more than 3% annually.[20]

Stradivari instruments are indeed rare and often today immensely valuable, if not today being close to priceless. They are usually musical instruments of legend.

---

[19] https://tarisio.com/cozio-archive/property/?ID=40262.
[20] http://content.time.com/time/business/article/0,8599,1903459,00.html

Chapter 9

How Many Strads Were Made?

"It is estimated that in total, Antonio Stradivari made around 1,100 musical instruments in total. This total is probably exaggerated according to Beare and Fulton. Of these, 600 (not all violins) are still thought to be in existence. Of that number, one source states only 244 violins are currently accounted for."[21] Wikipedia lists 248 known Stradivari violins.[22] Goodkind lists 635 Stradivari violins.[23] Most of these numbers are probably misleading. Estimates of known and accounted for Stradivari violins are widely inconsistent. The Goodkind number of 635 may be the most accurate.

The definitive work on Stradivari violins is the *Violin Iconography of Antonio Stradivari* by Herbert Goodkind who lists 635 Stradivari violins known but not necessarily accounted for entirely at the time of writing. This number is profoundly different from the estimates of 244 to 248 Wikipedia and other sources represent as being accounted for. E. Doring lists 440 known Strads and W.E. Hill 175. Mr. Goodkind's estimate of 635 is probably a more accurate figure, although a number of the Strads he lists have sketchy

---

[21] https://newviolinist.com/how-many-stradivarius-violins-are-there/.
[22] https://en.wikipedia.org/wiki/List_of_Stradivarius_instruments.
[23] Goodkind, Herbert. Violin Iconography of Antonio Stradivari. 1972 Self-published by Larchmont, New York.

provenances. Mr. Goodkind estimates that about 2,000 Stradivari instruments were originally made, and of these, about 800 original Stradivari violins.

Chapter 10

Authentications and Forgeries

Before Walter Hamma obtained a red Stradivari violin, we now know was *The Mendelssohn*, he would certainly have required authentication, and there was no one better qualified than Rembert to have provided authentication. In the rare-violin sales business, Rembert was truly an independent expert in the late 1920s to 1930s, and for many decades later.

Violins sold and authenticated by Wurlitzer retained a "Wurlitzer Number," a number glued inside the fiddle. Rembert put it in there so he could later identify the instruments. According to David Fulton, "The Wurlitzers always did that; the Hills always did that. Bein and Fushi also did that." [24]

The Wurlitzer stock cards reveal a great deal about an instrument. They would put on the stock card the history of the instrument as it passed through their hands, as well as what they paid and sold it for in a code. They encoded it so that someone glancing at the stock card couldn't necessarily tell what it sold for."[25] But Fulton knows the secret. Stock cards ensure authenticity.

---

[24] Visiting David Fulton, collector of Strads, del Gesùs and more.
https://www.violinist.com/blog/laurie/20175/21182/

[25] https://en.wikipedia.org/wiki/David_L._Fulton delete gap.

Mr. Fulton, with his database of Rembert records, was of help expanding the history of *The Mendelssohn*. Gaps still remained. He was of great help expanding the provenance of *La Pucelle of 1709.*

Although those who sold violins usually authenticated them, many authentications were false, because few dealers except for Rembert or Rudolph, and of course W.H. Hill and Hamma, were completely honest or had the knowledge and experience to determine authenticity accurately. It took a good ear too to confirm the authenticity of a Stradivarius sound.

Violins have been forged for generations. Violin forgery in the nineteenth century was an industry for hundreds of luthiers. Few individuals had the skills and ear necessary to determine if a so-called rare violin, specifically a Stradivari, was genuine. Rembert had those talents. So did Alfred Hill, Charles Beare and Robert Bein.

According to Fulton, "Strads are so well-made that they are virtually impossible to forge. That is not the case with del Gesùs. There are many forgeries of del Gesù." That is not to say that there are not many crude forgeries of both Strads and del Gesùs

Authentications from Rembert, whose integrity was untarnished and almost unmatched, were genuine, and so Rembert's (and Rudolph's) authentication would have been almost certainly necessary before Hamma bought an expensive Stradivari and especially a Stradivari violin with a 100-year gap, as known at the time, in known ownership. The resurrection of an unknown Stradivari violin with a significant breach in history undoubtedly aroused profound suspicion that it was a fake. These particulars give circumstantial weight to the argument that Rembert was involved with *The Mendelssohn* before Hamma obtained it – probably from Rembert himself.

Hamma would have been a fool to not have involved Rembert and Rudolph. Besides, who else would have been reliable authenticators? The Hills, well-known English, rare-violin dealers, did not speak fluent German, and Walter Hamma's first language was German. Rudolph spoke fluent German as his first language, and he and other Wurlitzers had long-time relationships with Hamma. Moreover, the Hills were, according to some commentators, anti-anything not English and anti-Semitic. Hamma was Jewish and probably mistrustful of anti-Semitics.

Rembert may not have entered *The Mendelssohn* into his own inventory Violins entered into inventories were meant to be sold. I suggest Rembert did not want his red violin entered into inventory, because he had no intentions of selling it, ever.

Goodkind lists four Stradivari violins of 1720 that a Wurlitzer had owned or sold on consignment. Goodkind's records included Rembert's records passed on to Goodkind by Marianne, the daughter of Rembert. These Stradivari violins were *The Bishop* or *Leveque*, the *Madrileno*, the *Bavarian*, and *The Woolhouse*. Goodkind does not list a Wurlitzer as having owned or sold *The Mendelssohn*. Clearly, Goodkind does not support any relationship between a Wurlitzer and *The Mendelssohn*. So, how could Goodkind and Marianne have been wrong?

In the play, I related what I think really happened without having total factual support. I suggest strongly Rembert never entered the red violin into his later Rembert Wurlitzer inventory because it was a "keeper," an instrument that held tremendous emotional value for him. Items entered into inventory were meant to be sold, and he did not want to sell his red violin. Ask yourself how likely it would be for your mother (or wife if, you are a man) to sell her wedding ring?

Elizabeth Pitcairn, the current owner of *The Mendelssohn,* is alleged to view her violin as "her life's most inspiring mentor and friend."[26] I respectfully and strongly suspect Rembert viewed the same violin with similar feelings.

In identifying a Stradivari forgery, a good ear was helpful, but not essential in recognizing the Stradivari sound, as when Rembert heard the red violin for the first time. The sound of the instrument enters only a little into determining authenticity. The sound of an instrument is greatly affected by condition, setup, the bow used, and whether or not a player is in touch with the instrument.

Oscilloscope sound patterns are not useful in confirming a Stradivari to be authentic. In the movie *The Red Violin,* oscilloscopes were used. That was misleading. Rembert did not use an oscilloscope.

All instruments that Antonio Stradivarius made bear a label written in Latin that reads, *"Antonius Stradivarius Cremonensis Faciebat Anno* [date]*."* The label indicated the maker, the place of production, and the date. Rembert glued a number inside each Stradivarius violin. Rather than demeaning the value of a Stradivarius, the Wurlitzer label added value, because it indicated Rembert Wurlitzer authentication.

The wood used by Stradivarius was usually maple infused with minerals. Some claim this infusion is the reason replication of sound has not been usually possible so far.[27] Others suggest it was how Antonio cut the "f" holes that creates the Stradivari sound.[28] Both aspects may contribute to a wonderful sound.

Identifying Stradivari forgeries is not easy or a totally trustworthy skill any more than identifying old master painting forgeries. On an often-cited occasion, Vuillaume made two copies of Paganini's Guarneri *"del Gesù," Il Cannone.* Paganini could not identify among

---

[26] Suzanne Marcus Fletcher alleged this in a program for a performance by Pitcairn with The Mendelssohn.

[27] https://www.asianscientist.com/2016/12/in-the-lab/stradivarius-violin-wood-mineral-preservative/.

[28] https://www.theregister.co.uk/2015/02/15/violin_acoustics_f_holes_mit/

the three violins his original *"del Gesù"* by craftsmanship or by sound.[29] Vuillaume made copies of *The Messiah*, and today there is widespread speculation, almost certainly unfounded, that *The Messiah* in the Ashmolean Museum of Art and Archaeology in Oxford is a Vuillaume forgery.[30] Even experts like W. Hill, Rudolph, or Rembert undoubtedly made mistakes in authentication that were sometimes left unrecorded, or better yet, corrected later.

---

[29] https://en.wikipedia.org/wiki/Il_Cannone_Guarnerius.
[30] The "widespread speculation" may be grandstanding by Stuart Pollens.

Chapter 11

How Many Stradivari Violins Did a Wurlitzer Find, Authenticate, Buy, or Sell on Consignment?

Through the auction house, Tarisio, that has an extensive record of Stradivari instruments, the *Violin Iconography of Antonio Stradivari* by Herbert Goodkind, and Mr. David Fulton, a rare musical instrument collector who has a copy of Wurlitzer stock card records compiled as a database, I have determined that a Wurlitzer, mostly Rembert, handled, authenticated, and sold, almost always on consignment, more than 158 Stradivari violins. Charles Beare, who had worked with Wurlitzer, actually recalled having seen more than one-hundred Stradivari violins during his apprenticeship at Wurlitzer.[31]

By some estimates, this 158 number was more than a quarter of all known and accounted-for Stradivari violins. Rembert had an amazingly refined and well-educated ear for Stradivari sounds. His acuity was so strong that he suspected an unknown, red violin was a Stradivarius just by hearing it played. To be sure, Rembert examined the instrument to confirm it was a Stradivarius.

---

[31] Freddie Beare reported this to Mr. David Fulton who reported this story in turn to the author.

Tarisio and Goodkind records were collated to determine how many records a Wurlitzer, either Rudolph, the father of Rembert, or Rembert himself had found. The number was 135. It was an incomplete number.

Mr. David Fulton examined the Rembert database and came up with 158 Stradivari violins that Rembert or a Wurlitzer had handled. Because it is not known when Wurlitzer started using stock cards, the total number could be significantly more than 158. In addition, Marianne Wurlitzer found a Stradivarius violin, the *Maia Bang*. Accordingly, a Wurlitzer found, bought or handled on consignment 158 or more Stradivari violins. That is an impressive number.

Rudolph Henry or Wurlitzer, led by Rembert's rare violin purchasing, bought and sold, some on consignment, about 42 Stradivari violins. Depending upon when Wurlitzer started using stock cards, some additional Stradivari might be added to the 158 number.

Rembert sold at least a hundred Stradivari violins independently after 1949 through the Rembert Wurlitzer Company to the best recollection of Freddie Beare who had worked with Rembert.. Goodkind often lists Wurlitzer as owner, consignee, or the seller as "Wurlitzer" without differentiating between Rembert and Rudolph or the ownership structure. Dealers such as W.H. Hill and Hamma may have handled as many rare instruments as Rembert or Wurlitzer, but their records are unavailable. It was never my intent to compare numbers of rare musical instruments various dealers handled.

At least 158 of all the known Antonio Stradivari violins in the world were held mostly on consignment at one time or another by Rembert or a Wurlitzer (either Rembert or Rudolph) where Rembert had been in charge of violin sales and purchases after 1926. Rudolph cannot be credited because of stock card uncertainties with any of the 42 Stradivari he handled, even though most of the early Wurlitzer purchases were at the direction of Rembert after 1926. So, almost all of the Stradivari violins handled or sold, mostly on consignment, by a Wurlitzer were by Rembert.

Nine violins of this 158 number may have included instruments made by Francesco and Omobono Stradivari, who were sons of Antonio. Technically, these nine were Stradivari, but not Antonio Stradivaris.

These facts may confirm Rembert had been one of the world's foremost rare violin authority and owner or consignee of the most Stradivari violins during his era. Hamma or W.H. Hill may have dealt with more rare musical instruments, but it is not my intent to compare numbers.

A list of the violins so far identified as having been handled or held by Wurlitzer (a.k.a. the Rudolph Wurlitzer Company or Wurlitzer Music Company) or Rembert is shown in Appendix 4. This list is incomplete, because it does not include the Fulton/Rembert database. As my research continues, I would not be surprised to identify more.

This brief study is a story of Rembert and the Stradivari that he loved and, in particular, *The Mendelssohn* of 1720 that the author claims he had owned and that violinist Elizabeth Pitcairn now owns. Among my personal memories, I refer to Rembert as the "Stradivarius Wurlitzer" just as there was a "Clarinet Wurlitzer" whom I met in East Germany and whose family, including Fritz and Herman historically, still makes clarinets today.[32] Furthermore, I respectfully suggest that *The Mendelssohn* of 1720 is the Red Violin my father told me about several times when I was a youth well before the movie *The Red Violin* ever emerged. My father was not an expert in violins, but he had a fantastic memory.

---

[32] https://wurlitzerklarinetten.de/clarinets/?lang=en.

It must have been very difficult for Rembert to certify alone the red violin as a Stradivari that had a 100-year or so gap in provenance at the time of its discovery. He may have called on his dad, Rudolph, for help, but there is no correspondence between them available to confirm this speculation.

Chapter 12

Fulton Coments

David Fulton is a recognized world expert on rare musical instruments, and in particular rare violins. He has collected many Stradivari instruments and is owner of a Rembert/Wurlitzer database containing many Wurlitzer transactions listed on stock cards. Through the stock cards, Mr. Fulton can access information about most instruments a Wurlitzer sold, bought, or had on consignment from the time stock cards were initiated and inventory started in this manner.

"At an unknown point, Wurlitzer started a practice of using "stock cards." These were cards that recorded sales prices in code, seller and buyer names, and provenance. Stock cards gave order to provenances.

Mr. David Fulton wrote in July 2020,
"Also, to my amazement, they took only a total of 197 Stradivari instruments altogether into inventory. Those, of course, were the Strads that were on consignment to be sold. I am certain Rembert certified lots of others and that is a gross underestimate of how many Stradivari instruments he examined. But only 197 were ever in inventory, and that's a solid figure."

"Here's the stock card breakdown:

158 Violins

3 Violas

16 Cellos

19 Labels – probably photographs of labels of some of the Strads they did not take into inventory but, perhaps, certified

1 Blank – used to add instruments to the database, not an instrument

------

197

So, there are actually 197 Stradivari instruments that are represented in the <Rembert or Wurlitzer> stock cards. Of that number 158 were Stradivari violins I think it would be fair to add the labels to the list, not as inventoried instruments but as instruments examined by Rembert and, quite probably, certified. I shouldn't be surprised if the label that appears in the 1720 Strad listing is, in fact, the label of *The Mendelssohn* Strad."

Question: As a matter of curiosity, does the 158 number of Stradivari violins Rembert handled according to the Rembert database include those Stradivari violins he handled when he worked for Wurlitzer before he formed his own company? Mr. Fulton replied, "That's the total number of Stradivari fiddles I have stock cards on. I have no idea when Wurlitzers started the stock card system for recording instruments and sales. Could have been before or after Rembert's era. I just don't know."

Question: Then the 158 number could theoretically include Stradivari violins Rudolph (Rembert's father) handled. "Yup. I can't rule that out. Don't have any idea when they started using the stock card system."

The answer then to the question how many Stradivari violins did Wurlitzers handle is at least 158.

Chapter 13

Resources

A resource used in this book, in addition to the Wikipedia list of Stradivari instruments, is the book *Stradivari* by Stewart Pollens. And still another resource is the previously mentioned, very expensive and exhaustive *Violin Iconography of Antonio Stradivari 1644-1737* with treatises on the life and work of the "Patriarch" of violinmakers including an inventory of 700 known or recorded Stradivari string instruments and an index of 3,500 names of past or present Stradivari owners and photographs of 400 Stradivari instruments with 1,500 views in cloth in a slipcase. This book was inscribed by Herbert K. Goodkind as a paperback in 1972. Goodkind's book is undoubtedly the most authoritative work today on Stradivari violins, and its inventory is far more extensive than the Tarisio database. My copy is autographed by Goodkind. A third resource was William Griess, grandson of Rudolph Henry Wurlitzer, who confirmed that the La Salle String Quartet performance program showed four instruments were made available by Rembert on September 20, 1953. Mr. Griess made a copy available to me of the Farny address in 1964 and reviewed this study as to its accuracy. A fourth source was Terry Hathaway, whose domain has been automatic musical instruments. Terry, who is an expert on Wurlitzer family history, reviewed this work also. A fifth source was the auction house Tarisio with their database taken off the Internet. A sixth, a particularly valuable resource, was Friederike Philipson from the Musikinstrumenten – the Museum Markneukirchen, who provided early photographs of Wurlitzers. She also confirmed Hamma's records were unavailable or no longer in existence. A seventh resource was Marianne Wurlitzer, the daughter of Rembert.

These principal resources collectively confirm the number of known Stradivari violins to be at least 248 and up to 635, and that Rembert or Wurlitzer handled and/or sold, mostly on consignment, 158 or more Stradivari violins at one time or another. The profound difference in numbers of Stradivari violins known and accounted for is indeed disturbing, but these differences are indisputable.

Goodkind's inventory is probably the most accurate, although it has errors as well, to wit, not listing Rembert being connected with the *La Pucelle of 1709* that he loaned to the La Salle String Quartet. There are other errors as well including those relating to *The Mendelssohn.*

As to who was one of the greatest collectors ever, it was Rembert, although he did not own all his Stradivari violins at the same time. Even Count Ignazio Alessandro Cozio di Salabue, often referred to as the supreme collector of violins, had only ten Stradivari violins,[33] and Luigi Tarisio who died in 1854 had twenty-four Stradivari violins in his estate after his death.[34] But dealers such as Hamma and W.H. Hills may have handled more violins than Rembert. I doubt anyone will ever know for sure.

The greatest collector today is Mr. Fulton. "Over the years he has owned eight Strads, eight del Gesùs, and 14 other instruments (violins,

---

[33] https://en.wikipedia.org/wiki/Ignazio_Alessandro_Cozio_di_Salabue.
[34] https://en.wikipedia.org/wiki/Luigi_Tarisio.

violas and cellos) with names such as Bergonzi, Guadagnini, Amati, Rugeri, Montagnana and Testore."[35]

The list at the end of this paper in Appendix 4 shows an incomplete breakdown from these sources of the Stradivari violins handled or held on consignment at different times by Rembert himself and by him and his dad Rudolph for the Wurlitzer Co. It has been difficult to develop a full list of Stradivari violins owned or on consignment at one time or another by Rembert, even using multiple resources, because so many records are incomplete, inaccurate, or unconsolidated, and sometimes differ from each other profoundly. It has been difficult to develop a case identifying unequivocally the red Stradivarius Rembert found probably in the late 1920s when my father was present.

After much research, I suspect Rembert or Wurlitzer owned or had on consignment at one time or another more than 158 Stradivari violins, including *La Pucelle*. After all, no one, a hundred years ago, I more than suspect, was so compulsive that records had to be always complete any more than an artist might compulsively keep track of all his or her paintings. Certainly, there are significant differences between Tarisio's and Goodkind's records and records compiled by other experts such as the Hammas', Henley, Hill, and Doring.[36] In fact, there is almost as much inconsistency as consistency.

In compiling the list of violins handled by Rembert based on the provenances provided by Tarisio Auction house, caution is warranted. Tarisio is named after the great violin collector, Luigi Tarisio, who died in 1854. After his death, the famous luthier and master violin forger, Jean-Baptiste Vuillaume, found 144 violins, including twenty-

---

[35] Visiting David Fulton, collector of Strads, del Gesùs and more. https://www.violinist.com/blog/laurie/20175/21182/

[36] Goodkind, H.K. *Violin Iconography of Antonio Stradivari*. Page 14.

four Stradivaris, in Luigi's attic.[37] Unfortunately, Luigi kept no records of any of his transactions, nor inventory of his collections. The auction house Tarisio now provides old provenances for many of the Tarisio/Vuillaume violins. Recent transactions and provenances of Stradivari violins are now better recorded including ownership by Rembert, but even Rembert's records as recorded by Goodkind when referencing old provenances are not infallible.[38]

---

[37] https://en.wikipedia.org/wiki/Luigi_Tarisio.
[38] https://tarisio.com/cozio-archive/cozio-carteggio/luigi-tarisio-part-1; and part 2.

Chapter 14

Provenance of the Red Violin

According to Elizabeth Pitcairn,[39] "An industrialist bought 'The Red Mendelssohn' in 1956 and owned it until it sold at an auction in 1990 for $1.7 million." That statement is partially inaccurate. The industrialist who bought the red violin in 1956 was Rembert in my opinion and as further supported by Tarisio for their violin #40316 known as *The Mendelssohn*. But Rembert did not sell the red violin in 1990, because he had died many years earlier in 1963.

According to Tarisio #40316 regarding *The Mendelssohn*, the industrialist who sold the violin in 1990 was either Rosenthal and Son, Schube, or Smith. Rembert could not have sold the red violin in 1968 or 1990, because he died in 1963. How could there be such confusion?

---

[39] https://pamplinmedia.com/pt/11-features/240821-107379-acclaimed-violinist-pitcairn-plays-with-famed-red-piece

Appendix 1
Tarisio Records

Tarisio #51374

The "Unnamed"

Provenance

Rembert Wurlitzer

Franz von Mendelssohn
Until 1968   Jacques Français

From 1968   Current owner

Certificate Jacques Francais NY, NY
1968 #929

Tarisio #40316

The Mendelssohn

Provenance

Lilli Von Mendelssohn

Until 1956 Hamma and Co.

From 1956 Rembert Wurlitzer

Until 1990 Luther Rosenthal

From 1990 Current owner

COMBINED RECORDS FROM GOODKIND, TARISIO, FULTON AND ME FROM 1913 TO PRESENT OF *THE MENDELSSOHN*

A partial list of rare instruments owned by Rembert is available at:

https://tarisio.com/cozio-archive/browse-the-archive/owners/?Entity_ID=9009

1913 to 1926 According to Mr. David Fulton, Francesco Mendelssohn was the owner of *The Mendelssohn* in 1913. Then Mr. Fulton's provenance shows a gap to 1990. After Francesco lost the fiddle, it may have passed through a number of hands, finally ending up with the gypsy who played the fiddle in an outside Berlin cafe when my father Raimund was present.

1926 Rembert Wurlitzer *Hamma was not the first owner after Francesco Mendelssohn. The author claims it was Rembert who sold the violin to Hamma.

From 1926 to 1956 Hamma

From 1956 to 1963 Rembert *Rembert died in 1963. Presumably his wife Lee had the violin briefly after 1963. It is not clear to whom she sold the fiddle, although possibly Rembert decided to sell it earlier. What seems clear is that Rembert was involved early in the twentieth century history of *The Mendelssohn* after Francesco Mendelssohn.

? To 1990 Jacques Français; Luther Rosenthal and son; Schube; Smith

These additional names are taken from Goodkind page 734 and added.

From 1990 Elizabeth Pitcairn

The Fulton provenance attached as Appendix 2 was also incomplete from 1913 until Pitcairn ownership in 1990. Mr. Fulton was of limited help in expanding upon this period. Note from 1913 to 1990, the Fulton provenance is completely undeveloped. In the book and play, I develop the provenance for that time period. It is entertaining that, according to Mr. Fulton, Francesco Mendelssohn owned the violin in 1913. So, how did *The Mendelssohn* get from Francesco to Rembert? I suggest how in the Prologue and the play itself.

As Mr. Fulton pointed out in a private email, there is no accurate way by examination of known records to prove or disprove Rembert found *The Mendelssohn*. My claim is that Rembert did find *The Mendelssohn*. The play develops that claim.

Hamma records are unavailable, at least to me, because his company is out of business. On my behalf, Friedericke Philipson of the Musikinstrumenten-Museum in Markneukirchen, near the ancestral home of Schöneck, contacted Hans Rehberg in Freudenstadt Obermusbach, who has researched the Hamma Family.

Unfortunately, Mr. Rehberg does not know where the documents of the company went and so could not be of help either in tracking down the history of *The Mendelssohn* further. Marianne Wurlitzer, the daughter of Rembert, could not be of help either. So, in part, this story of a Rembert red violin remains a mystery.

Walter Hamma working on a violin, possibly in the 1920s.

Walter Hamma was a colleague of Rembert

Mr. David Fulton is probably the greatest collector of rare musical instruments today. He has a copy of Rembert's database and unusual access to information about rare musical instruments. Mr. Fulton provided a provenance attached at the end of this book and play of *The Mendelssohn.*

The first recorded owner of *The Mendelssohn,* according to the Fulton provenance, is a Sig. Bernardo Darhan, sometime around 1850 or 1860. Then there is Francesco Mendelssohn in 1913 followed by Elizabeth Pitcairn in 1990. It is the intent of this book, in large part, to fill in the gaps from 1913 to 1990.

Filling in the gaps conclusively is not possible at this time. Mr. Fulton suggests Francesco Mendelssohn sold *The Mendelssohn* to Français, followed by Fred Smith, Rosenthal, and Max Verabay. If so, how did Hamma get in the ownership lineup? In my opinion, there were other intermediaries including Rembert. The provenance after Francesco Mendelssohn is quite incomplete. In any event, Francesco was notorious for losing Stradivari, not selling them.

Rembert bought *The Mendelssohn* in 1956 from Hamma, according to Tarisio #40316, and then sometime after 1956 and before his death in 1963, Rembert (or, if after 1963, his wife, Lee) sold *The Mendelssohn* to Luther Rosenthal and son.[40]

Although there is currently no irrefutable evidence that *The Mendelssohn* was the violin that Rembert discovered before Hamma obtained the violin, there is circumstantial evidence, namely the story my father told me about it being red in color – and there is still other evidence including the Tarisio accounting.

There is also a gap of about twenty years in provenance from the time of Felix Mendelssohn (1809-1847) to Sig. Bernando Darhan's ownership. When Rembert discovered the violin, there was a remarkable 100-year more-or-less gap.

---

[40] https://tarisio.com/cozio-archive/property/?ID=40316.

Rembert did not call the violin *The Mendelssohn*. He didn't know the history, and at the time he was not working for Wurlitzer. It was his violin. It did not have to be entered into Wurlitzer inventory. It was an unnamed Stradivarius Tarisio records as #51374. Since that violin can be shown to be *The Mendelssohn*, the provenance becomes more complete.

An unusual and very entertaining character in the provenance history of *The Mendelssohn* was the great nephew of Felix, Francesco Mendelssohn, who died in 1971. There is little doubt Francesco owned his namesake violin in 1913.

Rembert knew him very well, so well in fact that he lent Francesco a violin he had made in Mirecourt many years earlier. He pleaded with Francesco not to take his Stradivarius cello, *The Piatti*, with him on a trip. Francesco listened, fortunately, because a fire occurred in the dwelling where Francesco was staying and Rembert's violin was destroyed. A very valuable Stradivarius was saved. I wonder whether or not it was a drunken stupor that Francesco had which caused him to accidentally set the fire.

While the provenance was still incomplete, records somewhere had shown *The Mendelssohn*, and Joseph Joachim had owned it.[41] Rembert and his dad were good detectives when searching for the history of a rare musical instrument. At the time, there was little reason to publicize the discovery, and moreover, Rembert did not seek publicity. The red violin was, after all, just another Stradivarius, and Wurlitzer had owned or dealt with many.

The violin's provenance was certainly not immediately known. Circumstantial evidence, based primarily on my father's story and the

---

[41] The Pitcairn website cites Joachim as having owned *The Mendelssohn*. Marianne Wurlitzer and Mr. Fulton doubt Joachim owned *The Mendelssohn*.

deep, red color fairly uncommon[42] among rare Stradivari violins, and Tarisio renditions is that the red violin was *The Mendelssohn* and that the discoverer and authenticator was Rembert, possibly with the help of his dad, Rudolph Henry, also an authority on rare violins. Anthony Zatorski, speaking for Tarisio, informed me that they did not have the Rembert authentications that might have been of help in identifying the suspect violins and their histories further.

---

[42] The violins *Ruby Strad* and *The Sassoon* are also red Stradivari.

Appendix 2

Fulton Provenance Presented by Mr. David Fulton.

Violin

Antonio Stradivari
'Mendelssohn' 1720

BF S5684
RW
Hill

PROVENANCE		*Acquired through or from:*
		Notes on sources of info
1990	Elizabeth Pitcairn *	Christies
1913	Francesco Mendelssohn	
1913	Wilhelm Hermann Hammig	Bright
1901	Miss Bright	Kruse
1890	Prof Johann Kruse	Riechers
1890	August Riechers	Van Hal
1879	M. Van Hal	Germain
1878	Emile Germain	Pinteville
1863	Baron Pinteville	Gand
186?	C. N. Eugene Gand	Darhan (with Wilmotte Strad)
18??	Sig. Bernardo Darhan	

BIBLIOGRAPHY (* Illustrated)

2010 * Thone, Jost; Antonius Stradivarius 3 1990

* Christie's; Christie's Auction Nov 1990

lot 360

1990 * The Strad Magazine Nov 1990

1972 * Goodkind, Herbert K.; The Violin Iconography of Antonio Stradivari 1644-1737

1872 Gallay, Jules; Les Instruments des Ecoles Italiennes Gand, Freddie Eugene; Stradivarius - Guarnerius Del Gesù

as Pinteville; ex Garcia, ex Cadiz; 1879 Van Hal

Excerpts From Arthur F. Hill Diary

9/8/1891 Buziau also mentioned that one of the Strads. belonging to Mr. Van Hal, a professor at Brussels was bought in Paris for £160

3/9/1892 Kruser of Berlin, he tells me, has bought the Van Hal's Strad. off Reichers for £1000.

5/2/1892 C. Fletcher called and expressed a wish to buy the Roberts Strad. He mentioned that he thought the Strad. which has just been bought by Johann Kruse through Reichers of Berlin from M. Van Hals of Brussels was paid for by Lord St. Seven.

10/17/1895 Lady Anne Blunt, in the course of conversation, said that a cutting had appeared in the Westminster Gazette this week relative to the value of a Strad violin. It was little puff which evidently emanated from Prof. Kruse [krause?] in which it is stated that his Strad violin was worth £1,250, and in which it is compared to Prof. Joachim's. This is a violin that has been offered to Alfred, and that three or four years ago belonged to Mr. Van Hal, and if I recollect the price he wanted for it was about £600. Riechers, the German dealer, who died not long ago, purchased it or negociated its sale but nothing like £1,250 was ever spoken of as its value.

10/29/1897 Alfred and I went to call on Professor Kruse, who has left Berlin to settle in London. He has very good rooms at 66 St. James Street, and he evidently possesses means. We had quite a long talk, but at first I thought we should almost come to blows, as he tackled us over the general animus which he thinks we have against German fiddle makers. We showed him on what grounds we held these views, and told him many instances of their dreadful vandalism, and eventually he agreed with most of our remarks, and we parted very good friends. He showed me his Strad violin which is dated 1720. I have not seen it before, but I have often heard Alfred speak of it. It is a very fine type of Strad covered with a fine dark red varnish, and Kruse paid the sum of 22,000 Marks for it. Riechers, from whom he bought it, paid Mr. Van Hal of Brussels 19,000 Francs for it. However, he may have got it for less as Mr. Van Hal offered it to Alfred at a lower figure.

12/31/1897 Stradivari Kruse 29 Oct 1897

4/1/1901 Professor Kruse brought us his Strad today for repairs. He wishes us to put a new neck. We are very chary about doing such work for great artists, although compliment is paid us by their asking us to do it. They are so fanciful and without rhyme or reason are often dissatisfied with the going of their instruments.

6/15/1913 Amongst various other items of news, we gleaned from him that Miss Wietrowetz is now playing on the Stradivari which was formerly Kruse's, *The Mendelssohn*s having bought this instrument and lent it to her, it was one which Kruse's favourite pupil, Miss Bright, the daughter of the late Jacob Bright MP, played on for many years.

REMARKS

This violin belonged to an amateur, Senor Bernardo Darhan. He was a pupil of Lafont and no doubt purchased the violin in Paris through his intermediary, he lived at Cadiz and retained the instrument for many years finally selling it together with a second example about 1860 - 65 to Gand freres for 7, 000 frs. Gand immediately passed one on to Wilmotte of Antwerp for 3, 500 frs. and retained the other subsequently disposing of it in 1863 to Baron Pinteville of Paris for 4200 frs. From the latter it passed 1878 to the hands of Germain (he paid 7500 frs.) who sold it to M. Van Hal of Brussels in 1879 for 14000 frs. In 1890 Riechers purchased it from the last named owner for 19000 frs. and resold it to Kruse for 12000 marks (£1100 this violin was lent for sometime by Van Hal to Hubay, the violinist). Sold by Kruse to Miss Bright for £1100 (K would not take a profit) about the autumn of 1901. Sold to Hammig of Berlin no doubt on the advice of Kruse 1913 - 14 and it is now owned by the Mendelsohns (I believe Franz M.)

PRESERVATION

Excellent - belly underedged (done by Riechers of Berlin) a crack descends from top to bottom on right hand side, slight one at right top side - otherwise so far as I could discern sound. In character this instrument resembles the "Maurin Strad " - model rather flatter, head neat and the back has been trimmed away somewhat by a vandal. I note the right F is higher than the left.

DIMENSIONS
Length 14"
Width 8¼ - 6 and 5/8
Sides 1¼ - 1.3/16ths

WOOD

...of back in two, broad wavy curl descending, sides, though plainer match - belly of open grain at flanks - head plain.

VARNISH

...of plum red colour, the whole fairly well covered that on back picturesquely worn, it has been slightly retouched.

ANTONIO STRADIVARI: A VIOLIN KNOWN AS *THE MENDELSSOHN* OR RED MENDELSSOHN *OF 1720*. CREMONA.

Violinist Elizabeth Pitcairn is the owner of the 1720 Stradivari known as *The Mendelssohn*. Purchased at Christie's London salesrooms in 1990 for $1,700,000, it was at the time the world auction record for a work by Stradivari. The violin appeared to vanish after 1913 when it was owned by Francesco Mendessohn until I suggest it was discovered by Rembert in the 1920s in Berlin. Unfortunately, after writing her, Pitcairn could not be of help in developing the provenance of *The Mendelssohn* further.

Rembert, or another Wurlitzer, and my father would sometimes stop in Berlin. I have old, undated photos showing my father in Berlin sometime in the mid- or late-1920s before his father and my grandfather Howard died in 1928. It was on one of these trips I speculate that my father joined Rembert at a Berlin beer restaurant where a gypsy planed a red violin. My father left Wurlitzer in 1928 after his father, Howard, CEO of Wurlitzer, died.

Canadian filmmaker Francois Girard's imaginative speculations about *The Mendelssohn* and its 1990 Christie's auction became the narrative for the 1999 Academy Award-winning film, *The Red Violin*. Literally, none of the past history was known initially about *The Mendelssohn* after its resurrection in the 1920s.

In a program for a performance by Pitcairn with *The Mendelssohn*, Suzanne Marcus Fletcher wrote: "The historic violin was crafted in 1720 by Antonio Stradivari, who lovingly made his instruments in his small shop in Cremona, Italy centuries ago, and remains the most famous violin maker of all time. Not long after its creation, the instrument appeared to vanish; no one knows where or to whom the violin belonged for more than 200 years,[43] spawning any number of historians, writers, journalists, critics as well as Canadian filmmaker, Francois Girard, to speculate on the violin's mysterious history. Girard's imaginative speculations became the narrative for his beloved film, *The Red Violin*."

"Known as the *Red Stradivarius* and owned by legendary violinist Joseph Joachim, the 1720 *Red Mendelssohn* Stradivarius would eventually surface in 1920s Berlin. It had been purchased by an heir to the great composer, Felix Mendelssohn. In 1956, it was purchased by a New York industrialist (presumably referring to Rembert, as Tarisio records for #40316 probably confirm) who kept the instrument in impeccable performance condition. Much of its original burnished red varnish remains on the violin today, and it is thought to be one of the best sounding and most beautiful of Stradivari's remaining violins. Then on Thanksgiving Day in 1990, the instrument's fate would once again be triggered when the industrialist (presumably referring to Rosenthal, Schube or Smith[44]) opted to put the Red Stradivarius on the auction block anonymously at Christie's of London. While some of the world's most powerful sought to win the coveted instrument, it landed in the hands of then sixteen-year-old American solo violinist, Elizabeth Pitcairn. Pitcairn would remain silent about owning the violin until her rapidly

---

[43] Two hundred years is incorrect. It was more like 100 years. Remember, please, the author did not write this blurb.

[44] Goodkind, H.K. *Violin Iconography of Antonio Stradivari*. Page 734

burgeoning solo career brought her into the public eye on international concert stages after nearly three decades of rigorous training by the world's most esteemed violin teachers."

"Pitcairn would come to view the violin as her life's most inspiring mentor and friend. Many have said that the violin has finally found its true soul mate in the gifted hands of the young violinist who is the first known solo artist to ever bring it to the great concert halls of the world, and who has made it her goal to share the violin's magical beauty of sound with people of all ages, professions, and cultures. Today, Pitcairn and the *Red Mendelssohn* Stradivarius violin continue to foster one of classical music's most compelling partnerships." – **By Suzanne Marcus Fletcher**

The story about *The Mendelssohn* continues. Now the violin is listed in the auction house Tarisio's inventory in New York as item #40316.[45]

The provenance is interesting as cited by Tarisio and provocative as modified by me:

---

[45] https://tarisio.com/cozio-archive/property/?ID=40316.

Appendix 3

Combined Provenance from All Sources of *The Mendelssohn*

1. **Lilli von *Mendelssohn***

2. **Franz von *Mendelssohn* (1809 – 1847)**

    So where did the violin go after Felix? Who owned it after *The Mendelssohn*s is partly speculation.

3. **Joseph Joachim**, the legendary violinist, dates unknown. Elizabeth Pitcairn lists Joachim as an owner.

    …a 20-year gap?

4. 18??   Sig. Bernardo Darhan
5. 186? C. N. Eugene Gand   Darhan (with Wilmotte Strad)
6. 1863 Baron Pinteville Gand
7. 1878 Emile Germain Pinteville
8. 1879 M. Van Hal Germain
9. 1890 August Riechers Van Hal
10. 1890 Prof Johann Kruse Riechers
11. 1901 Miss Bright Kruse
12. 1913   Wilhelm Hermann Hammig   Bright
13. 1913   Francesco Mendelssohn

    How did *The Mendelssohn* pass from Francesco? Read the play to find out.

14. **Rembert Wurlitzer? Early 1926?**

(*The Mendelssohn* or *The Red Violin* was found probably, in my opinion, sometime in the mid- or late-1920s in Berlin by Rembert before my father left Wurlitzer in 1928, since my father was with Rembert when he found a red violin. Nonetheless, it could have been in the 1930s. A very likely date is 1926 before Rembert, at the age of 22, was made head of Wurlitzer acquisitions, I suspect, in large part as a reward for having found a red Stradivarius violin. That violin was almost certainly *The Mendelssohn*, as it was later called.)

Tarisio lists Rembert as having been the first owner of its Stradivarius violin #51374, one of the suspects as having been the real *Red Violin*.

Rembert would then have authenticated the red violin perhaps with his father, Rudolph Henry, who had gone to a violin school in Berlin. Then, I suggest, Rembert sold the violin at an unknown date to Hamma, later in 1926 or even less likely in the 1930s.

According to Tarisio, Rembert purchased *The Mendelssohn* violin (Tarisio #40316) from Hamma in 1956. There could have been a later authentication as well if Rembert sold the violin to Luther Rosenthal and Son sometime after 1956. Since Rembert died in 1963, it was probably Rembert's wife, Lee, who sold a red violin then. This somewhat speculative outline is expanded upon in Addenda III and IV.

15. Hamma and Co., until 1956

Hamma records as to who sold him *The Mendelssohn* are unavailable. I suggest it was Rembert who found this legendary red violin, authenticated it with the help of his father Rudolph, a world-recognized rare violin expert, and then sold it to Walter Hamma in the mid or later 1920s, but before 1928 when my father left Wurlitzer shortly after his father Howard had died.

Publicity was unimportant. I suggest further Hamma would never have agreed to buy the violin originally around 1926 up to 1928 without Wurlitzer authentication from the world's two foremost experts, Rembert and Rudolph Henry, giving further circumstantial support that Rembert was involved with the violin at a very early point after its resurrection in the 1920s.

Unfortunately, there is no known written record today, to the best of my knowledge, of how Hamma obtained the violin to confirm my story. Tarisio affirms Rembert was the first owner of the red, unnamed Stradivarius #51374, but Herr Hamma is not listed as an owner after Rembert.

Admittedly, I have entered into speculation, but it is speculation based on common sense and knowledge of many particulars. The circumstantial evidence is very convincing Rembert owned a red Stradivarius violin of 1720. None of the four Stradivari violins of 1720 listed by Goodkind to have been handled by a Wurlitzer were recorded to have been red. Nonetheless, *The Unnamed* Tarisio #51734 remains a prime suspect.

16. **Rembert Wurlitzer,** from 1956 until 1963 when he died. Tarisio records for *The Mendelssohn* Tarisio #40316 list Rembert having become an owner in 1956. Since Rembert died in 1963, he could not have sold the violin in 1968. Presumably, his wife Lee sold the violin in 1968. Luthier Rosental and Son, Schube and Smith were later owners according to Goodkind.

17. **Lee Wurlitzer**, from 1963 to 1968. In 1968, Lee, the widow of Rembert, sold a red violin Tarisio #51374 to Jacques Francais, et al. Perhaps, Lee also sold *The Mendelssohn* that same year to Jacques Francais. Goodkind does not give dates.

18. **Jacques Francais** from 1968? to ? Luthier Rosenthal and Son, Schube and Smith are listed by Goodkind also as owners. They may have been co-owners. Collating information from Tarisio and other records is not easy.

19. **Luthier Rosenthal** ? to ? Dates are unavailable.

20. **Shube and then Smith,** ????. Goodkind lists these individuals as owners after Jacques Francais. It is surprising that relatively recent transactions are not recorded well.

Since Rembert passed away in 1963, Rembert could not have had the violin personally up to 1990 as the Tarisio provenance suggests for violins #40316. This inconsistency is just another example of how provenances are often incomplete.

Luther Rosenthal and Son, or Schube, and then Smith???, from around 1968 until 1990. Goodkind does not give dates for owners.

21. **Elizabeth Pitcairn,** from 1990 through Christies and Current Owner,
    Tarisio does not even list Pitcairn as a current owner.

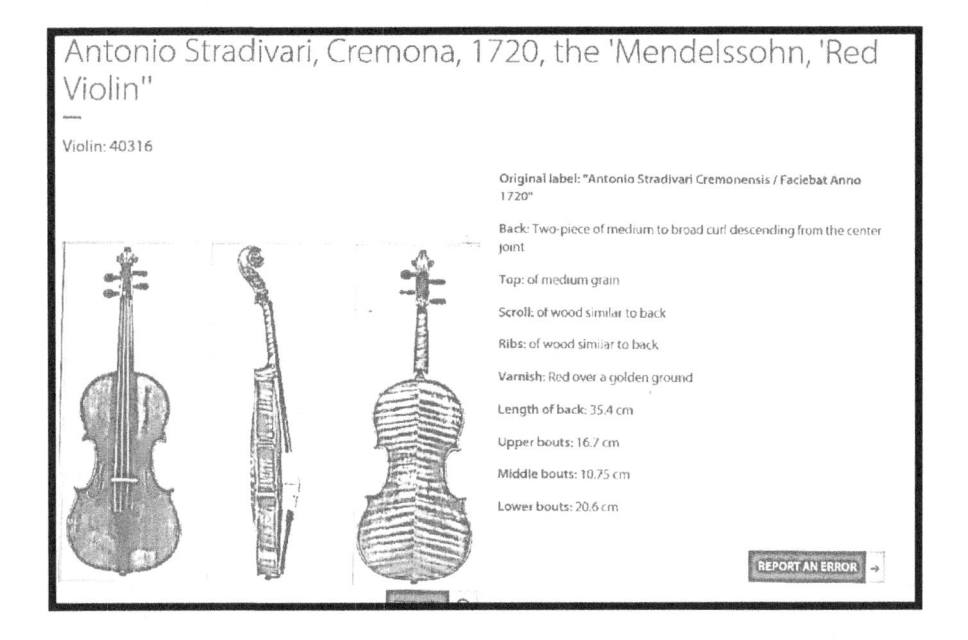

> **Antonio Stradivari, Cremona, 1720, the 'Mendelssohn,' 'Red Violin"**
>
> Violin: 40316
>
> Original label: "Antonio Stradivari Cremonensis / Faciebat Anno 1720"
>
> Back: Two-piece of medium to broad curl descending from the center joint
>
> Top: of medium grain
>
> Scroll: of wood similar to back
>
> Ribs: of wood similar to back
>
> Varnish: Red over a golden ground
>
> Length of back: 35.4 cm
>
> Upper bouts: 16.7 cm
>
> Middle bouts: 10.75 cm
>
> Lower bouts: 20.6 cm
>
> REPORT AN ERROR →

Tarisio Website

Unfortunately, Tarisio does not have the original authentications that might have helped in confirming provenance further.

More than once, Rembert bought, sold, and then bought the same violin again as, for example, the *Baron Knoop* of 1715. The psychology that can be added to circumstantial arguments may be that it was easier for Rembert to buy in 1956 a violin he had already authenticated than one not previously authenticated by him. Walter Hamma may also have felt it was easier and more practical, or even that he was morally obligated, to sell *The Mendelssohn* in 1956 to Rembert, an eager buyer who had discovered and authenticated it. Rembert had the money and was well known for being fair. Stradivari are rarely bought or sold at bargain prices.

There is no other history known to me of ownership coming close to Rembert's record ever for owning or controlling through consignments Stradivari instruments, although admittedly, Rembert did not obviously own or control all these Stradivari violins at the same time. This fact that Rembert owned, handled or sold unequivocally an extraordinary number of Stradivari violins qualifies calling Rembert "The Stradivarius Wurlitzer." If W.H. Hill, Hamma, or any other dealer can be shown to have handled more violins I would defer to them and call that dealer, "The Stradivarius Dealer."

The evidence that Rembert discovered *The Mendelssohn* in the 1920s is very convincing. But if proof surfaces otherwise that *The Mendelssohn* was not discovered by Rembert sometime in the 1920s or even in the 1930s, then I would withdraw my suggested change in provenance, although insisting that the story of a red violin found by Rembert as related to me by my father was true and not hearsay. Then my question would be, what red Stradivari violin was it that Rembert discovered in the 1920s?

Appendix 4

An Incomplete List of 135[46] Stradivari Violins Owned or Sold by a Wurlitzer According to Goodkind and Tarisio

This list is not the list of 158 Stradivari violins in the Fulton/Rembert database. That list was unavailable to the author. It is a list created by collating information from Tarisio and Goodkind.

What is of interest is those Stradivari violins handled by the Wurlitzer Music Company. The 42 number of violins handled by Rudolph cannot be added to the 158 Stradivari violins in the Rembert database owned by Mr. David Fulton, because we do not know when Wurlitzer started using stock cards. The true number is probably significantly larger. There were instances possibly though when the same violin was handled a second time with a second stock card.

The first two violins marked with an asterisk (*) have had their provenances revised. Caveats exist, so bear with me please.

More credence was given to Goodkind than to Tarisio because of the obvious thoroughness and scholarship of Goodkind. Moreover, Goodkind was a personal friend of Rembert, visiting him often. Goodkind had greater access to Rembert than Tarisio auction house.

Although Tarisio had far fewer references to Stradivari violins than Goodkind, I believe a fairly exhaustive list was created by collating my two primary sources, Tarisio and Goodkind, for Stradivari violins handled or sold by a Wurlitzer. That is not to say I am representing the list is conclusive. Repeated efforts were taken to avoid duplications and to be accurate.

---

[46] 136 Stradivari violins are listed, but two violins are the same as explained shortly in the Apology, making the number 135. Actually, Marianne Wurlitzer sold a Stradivarius that is not listed, but is referenced in the play *Rembert* that follows.

When both Tarisio and Goodkind reported a Stradivari violin to have been owned by a Wurlitzer, there should be little doubt in the authenticity of that mutual representation. It remains odd, though, that there should be so many discrepancies. Countless times, Goodkind would list Wurlitzer as an owner or seller, while Tarisio would not confirm this representation, and vice versa.

This listing of Stradivari violins handled or sold by a Wurlitzer has been very time-consuming. One of the barriers to entry of undertaking this task was the expense of the Goodkind book running up to a thousand dollars or more. I was fortunate to obtain an autographed Goodkind book of his *Violin Iconography of Antonio Stradivari*. Without doubt, the Goodkind book has the most exhaustive list of Stradivari violins of any book published on the subject.

Abbreviations

WNLT = Wurlitzer Not Listed by Tarisio; WNLG = Wurlitzer Not Listed by Goodkind
(S) = Sold by Wurlitzer, not necessarily owned; Goodkind/T = Listed by both Goodkind and Tarisio

Year	Sobriquet	Provenance	Notes or Tarisio #
Antionio Stradivari Violins			
1720	*The Mendelssohn**	Lilli von Mendelssohn	40316
		Franz von Mendelssohn	
	The Provenance has been presented in Chapter 8		

Year	Sobriquet	Provenance	Notes or Tarisio #
1709	*La Pucelle* *	Freddie Herman	40212
		Until 1851 Jean-Baptiste Vuillaume	
		in 1870 Glandaz	
		In 1878 Sold by Hotel Drouot	
		From 1878 Unknown	
		In 1903 Sold by Caressa & Francais	
		1903-1904 W.E. Hill & Sons	
		From 1904 Richard C. Baker	
		Until 1942 W.E. Hill & Sons	
		1942-1946 Robert Augustus Bower	
		From 1946 Frank Otwell	

	Not listed on Tarisio	**1953 Rembert Wurlitzer?**	Loaned to La Salle Sept. 20, 1953 on consignment. Bought on 5/11/1955
		1956 Anna E. Clark	
		Huguette M. Clark Rembert 1955	
		From 2001 David L. Fulton. Fulton Foundation sold it 2019 for $22 million	
1679	***The Hellier***	Rembert Wurlitzer	40237
1681	***Chanot-Chardon***	Goodkind/T	41488
1681	***Reynier***	Goodkind/T Rudolph	40675
1682	***Hill, Banat***	Rembert Wurlitzer	41257
1683	***Martinelli, Gingold***	Rudolph Wurlitzer	40473
1683	***Madame Bastard***	Wurlitzer by Goodkind	WNLT
1684	***Soames***	Goodkind/T Rudolph	40742
1685	***MacKenzie, Castelbarco***	Rembert Wurlitzer	40756
1685	***Becker; Florentiner***	Goodkind/T Rudolph	40750
1685	***Marquis***	Goodkind/T Rudolph	40470
1687	***Marie Law***	Wurlitzer by Goodkind	41431

1688	*Derenberg*	Rembert Wurlitzer	40760
1690	*The Theodor*	Rembert Wurlitzer	41446
1690	*Stephens*	Goodkind/T Rudolph	40726
1693	*Harrison*	Rembert Wurlitzer	40039
1694	*Irish, Burgundy, St. Sebastian*	Rembert Wurlitzer	40783
1695	*Goetz; Hawaiian*	Goodkind/T Rudolph	40785
1696	*Vornbaum, Weinberger*	Wurlitzer by Goodkind	WNLT
1697	*Montbel*	Rembert Wurlitzer	41321
1697	*Uchtomsky*	Goodkind/T Rudolph	41263
1698	*Lark*	Goodkind/T Rudolph	41266
1698	*Schumann*	Goodkind/T Rudolph	40472
1698	*Greiner*	Goodkind/T Rudolph	WNLT
1698	*Joachim;Kortschalk*	Goodkind/T Rudolph	40474
1699	*Contesssa, de Polignac*	Rembert Wurlitzer	40125
1699	*La Font #1*	Goodkind/T Rudolph	40274
1700	*Jupiter*	Rudolph Wurlitzer	41306
1700	*Taft; van Donop; Ward*	Wurlitzer by Goodkind	40116
1701	*Circle*	Wurlitzer by Goodkind	41312
1701	*Johnson, Dushkin, Sandler*	Goodkind/T Rudolph	40079

1702	*King Maximilian Joseph*	Rembert Wurlitzer	40080
1703	*Alsager*	Goodkind/T Rudolph	41318
1703	*Montbel*	Goodkind/T Rudolph	41321
1703	*de Rougement #1*	Wurlitzer by Goodkind	40478
1703	*de Rougement #2, Ford*	Goodkind/T Rudolph	40257
1704	*Betts*	Goodkind/T Rudolph	40118
1704	*Viotti*	Wurlitzer by Goodkind	41327
1705	*Baron von der Leyen*	Rembert Wurlitzer	31299
1707	*The Hammer*	Rembert Wurlitzer	40643
1707	*Dragonetti; Rivaz*	Wurlitzer by Goodkind	40057
1708	*The Ruby*	Rembert Wurlitzer	40084
1708	*Balakovic, Soll, Strauss*	Wurlitzer by Goodkind	41156
1708	*Dancla*	Wurlitzer by Goodkind	43076
1708	*Huggins*	Goodkind/T Rudolph	40053
1709	*Ernst*	Goodkind/T Rudolph	40287
1709	*Siberian; The Jack*	Goodkind/T Rudolph	41350
1710	*MacKenzie, Castelbarco*	Rembert Wurlitzer	40756
1710	*Berger, Dancla*	Goodkind/T Rudolph	43077
1711	*Earl of Plymouth, Kreisler*	Rembert Wurlitzer	44058

1712	**Darnley, Eldina Bligh**	Rudolph Wurlitzer	41371
1712	**Hrimali, Press**	Rembert Wurlitzer	41378
1712	**Viotti**	Wurlitzer by Goodkind	40288
1713	**Gaglione; Hill**	Wurlitzer by Goodkind	WNLT
1713	**Soncy; Kubelik**	Wurlitzer by Goodkind	40491
1713	**Rodewald**	Wurlitzer by Goodkind	WNLT
1713	**Pingrille**	Wurlitzer by Goodkind	40492
1713	**Havemeyer**	Wurlitzer by Goodkind	WNLT
1714	**Kneisel, Grun**	Rembert Wurlitzer	23286
1714	**Dolphin or Delfino**	Rembert Wurlitzer	29483
1714	**Joachim Ma**	Rembert Wurlitzer	40496
1714	**Adam**	Wurlitzer by Goodkind	41383
1715	**Lipinski**	Rembert Wurlitzer	40497
1715	**Baron Knoop, Bevan**	Rembert Wurlitzer	41471
1715	**The Lipinski**	Rembert Wurlitzer	40497
1715	**Hochstein**	Wurlitzer by Goodkind	41390
1715	**Titian**	Goodkind/T Rudolph	41393
1716	**Otto Booth, Cho-Ming Sin**	Rembert Wurlitzer	40057
1716	**Cessole**	Rembert Wurlitzer	41398

1716	*The Serdet*	Rembert Wurlitzer	41967
1717	*The Reiffenberg*	Rembert Wurlitzer	41538
1717	*Duchess*	Wurlitzer by Goodkind	WNLT
1717	*Fite; Windsor*	Wurlitzer by Goodkind	40439
1717	*Gariel*	Wurlitzer by Goodkind	41424
1717	*Matthews*	Wurlitzer by Goodkind	WNLT
1717	*Mercadente*	Wurlitzer by Goodkind	WNLT
1717	*Piatti*	Goodkind/T Rudolph	40503
1717	*Toenniges*	Wurlitzer by Goodkind	WNLT
1718	*Mylnarski*	Wurlitzer by Goodkind	41478
1718	*Tyrell; Speyer*	Wurlitzer by Goodkind	40508
1718	*Wilmotte*	Goodkind/T Rudolph	43091
1719	*Wickett; Wurlitzer*	Wurlitzer by Goodkind	WNLT
1720	*Bavarian*	Rembert Wurlitzer	41488
1720	*Unnamed*	Rembert Wurlitzer	51374
1720	*L'Eveque*	Goodkind/T Rudolph	40517
1720	*Madrileno*	Goodkind/T Rudolph	43093
1720	*Woolhouse*	Wurlitzer by Goodkind	41489
1721	*The Mercadent*	Rembert Wurlitzer	43086

1721	Archinto	Goodkind/T Rudolph	41500
1721	Vidoudez, Maazel, Artol	Wurlitzer by Goodkind	40210
1722	Cadiz; Cannon; Wilmotte	Wurlitzer by Goodkind	40527
1722	de Chapenay	Wurlitzer by Goodkind	40291
1722	Earl of Westmorland	Goodkind/T Rudolph	40523
1722	Elman	Wurlitzer by Goodkind	41503
1723	Kiesewetter	Rembert Wurlitzer	40085
1723	Joachim, Elman	Goodkind/T Rudolph	41503
1723	McCormack; Edler	Goodkind/T Rudolph	41514
1725	The Koeber	Rembert Wurlitzer	43099
1725	Bott; Cambridge	Goodkind/T Rudolph	40528
1725	Lubbock	Goodkind/T Rudolph	41520
1725	Wilhelm	Wurlitzer by Goodkind	40060
1727	Kreutzer	Goodkind/T Rudolph	40535
1727	The Venus	Rembert Wurlitzer	41530
1727	DuPont	Wurlitzer by Goodkind	41154
1727	Smith; Wendling; Barrett	Wurlitzer by Goodkind	41546
1727	Venus; Cho-Ming Sin	Wurlitzer by Goodkind	WNLT

1728	*Villefranche*	Wurlitzer by Goodkind	WNLT
1729	*Benny; Artot Alard*	Wurlitzer by Goodkind	43102
1729	*Libon; Stuart; Dickinson*	Wurlitzer by Goodkind	41544
1730	*Johnson; Royal Spanish*	Wurlitzer by Goodkind	49637
1731	*Garcin*	Wurlitzer by Goodkind	41500
1731	*Romanoff; Maurin*	Wurlitzer by Goodkind	40249
1732	*Alcontara*	Goodkind/T Rudolph	41405
1732	*Taylor*	Goodkind/T Rudolph	40541
1733	*des Rossiers*	Goodkind/T Rudolph	40677
1734	*Lam, Scotland*	Rembert Wurlitzer	41367
1734	*Ames*	Wurlitzer by Goodkind	40545
1734	*Amherst*	Goodkind/T Rudolph	40544
1734	*Scotland University*	Wurlitzer by Goodkind	41567
1735	*Nestor, Leveque, Rode*	Rembert Wurlitzer	40533
1735	*Lamoureux*	Goodkind/T Rudolph	40546
1736	*Doria, Armingaud*	Rembert Wurlitzer	43108
1737	*Swan Song*	Rudolph Wurlitzer	40540
1737	*Lord Norton*	Rembert Wurlitzer	41574
1737	*d'Armaille*	Wurlitzer by Goodkind	41575

1737	**Norton**	Wurlitzer by Goodkind	41574
1743	**Baron Knoop**	Rembert Wurlitzer	41411

Nine Sons of Stradivari Violins Owned by Rembert			
Year	Maker (Stradivari)	Sobriquet	Source	Tarisio #
1734	Francesco	*TC Peterson*	Wurlitzer by Goodkind	45521
1736	Omobono	*?*	Rembert Wurlitzer	43108
1738	Omobono	*Tanocky Kazarian*	Wurlitzer by Goodkind	41595
1740	Omobono	*Zarontin*	Wurlitzer by Goodkind	None
1740	Omobono	*Weiner; Paul*	Wurlitzer by Goodkind	43114
1740	Omobono	*Frecke*	Wurlitzer by Goodkind	None
1740	Omobono	*Gulina*	Wurlitzer by Goodkind	None
1740	Omobono	*Leveque*	Wurlitzer by Goodkind	None
1742	Francesco	*Le Besque*	Rembert Wurlitzer	42845

Appendix 5
Bibliography

1. *Stradivari* by Stewart Pollens. Cambridge University Press 2010. This is an exhaustively researched book with details about Stradivari manufacturing that may overwhelm readers because of the thoroughness. Beautifully colored photos of some Stradivari are included. Provenances are very sketchy.

2. "*Violin Iconography of Antonio Stradivari. 1644-1737.* Treatises on the Life and Work of the "Patriarch" of Violinmakers. Inventory of 700 Known or Recorded Stradivari String Instruments." Index of 3,500 Names of Past or Present Stradivari Owners. Photographs of 400 Stradivari instruments with 1,500 Views. 1972. Cloth in slipcase. Inscribed by Herbert K. Goodkind with TLS. Paperback – 1972. This is a very pricey book that costs usually $600 U.S. or more. Its index is marvelous and far more extensive than the Tarisio records.

3. *The Rainaldi Quartet*: Gianni & Gustafest #1 (Giannia & Gustafeste) by Paul Adam July 1, 2007.

4. *Stradivari's Genius: Five Violins, One Cello* by Tony Faber

5. *Antonio Stradivari – the Celebrated Violin Maker* by Francois-Joseph Fétis. 2013 Dover Publications.

6. *The Violin: A Social History of the World's Most Versatile Instrument* by David Schoenbaum. Hardcover

7. *Violins of Hope:* Violins of the Holocaust--Instruments of Hope and Liberation in Mankind's Darkest... by James A. Grymes Paperback

8. *The Violin Maker:* Finding a Centuries-Old Tradition in a Brooklyn Workshop, Marchese, John
9. *Known Violin Makers* 7th Edition by John H. Fairfield, self-published. This book is fascinating to me because of citations of early Wurlitzer music instrument makers.
10. *A Thousand Mornings of Music* by Arnold Gingrich
11. Tariso auction house inventories at tarisio.com
12. Wikipedia List of Stradavari musical instruments at https://en.wikipedia.org/wiki/List_of_Stradivarius_instruments
13. William Griess, Grandson of Rudolph Henry Wurlitzer. Proofreader and information contributor.
14. *The Wurlitzer Family Grave Sites* by Terry Hathaway, an expert on automated music instruments. Published by Mechanicalmusicpress.
15. Friedericke Philipson of the Musikinstrumenten-Museum in Markneukirchen
16. *The Lady of the Casa, The Biography of Helene V.B. Wurlitzer* by John Scolie. The Rydal Press, 1959.
17. *Wurlitzer Family History* by Lloyd Graham 1955
18. *Antonio Stradivari – His Life and Work (1644 – 1737)* by W. Hill, Arthur Hill and Alfred Hill. 1965 by Dover Publications.
19. *Wurlitzer Family History* by Lloyd Graham May 1955 Published by Always Junkin'
20. *Wurlitzer of Cincinnati – The Name that Means Music to Millions* by Mark Palkovic. 2015 Published by the History Press.

21. Private correspondence with Marianne Wurlitzer, daughter of Rembert Wurlitzer
22. *The Violin Maker – Finding a Centuries-Old Tradition In A Brooklyn Workshop* by John Marchese. HarperCollings Publishers 2007
23. Private correspondence with Mr. David Fulton of Seattle in June 2020.
24. *Adventures of a Cello* by Carlos Prieto. University of Texas Press. October 1, 2006
25. *Stradivari, his Life and Work* by Hill 1902

Addendum 1
Epilogue

This entire book with play was written as a history of Rembert Wurlitzer, a young man who discovered a red Stradivarius, and who, over time, became obsessed with rare violins.

Along the way of my journey writing a detective story about Rembert, I felt that my story could not be finished without completing a play or short story. Poetic license was taken in writing a play based on real and circumstantial evidence. It became my first attempt at writing a play.

In the play or short story, facts fit together very well with speculation. The actual year Rembert found the red violin could have been 1925 as well as 1926, but surely before Howard died and my father left Wurlitzer in 1928.

The play presented earlier simply called *Rembert* outlines what I think really happened using circumstantial and real evidence presented in the book. It is a play that follows Rembert from the time he went to Princeton to his death caused by a heart attack at age 59.

Although based mostly on facts, the play *Rembert* is still very much a speculative journey following Rembert's life through imagined conversations at important turning points in his life.

Poetic license was taken as I projected through dialogue and timelines what really happened in my opinion. I suggest that in many ways the play is more realistic and true to life than the recorded history, which is clouded by innumerable inconsistencies in recorded inventories by Rembert, Goodkind and others of Stradivari violins.

Because of the quarantine imposed by COVID-19, I became tired of television and reading and found time to write. Without a COVID-19 quarantine, I doubt I would have written the book and the play. Then I would have been left with an unease that my father's story about Rembert finding a red violin had never been developed into a play. Writing the play saved me from going stir-crazy.

I hope you have enjoyed the short story or play and the book.

Fred Wurlitzer April 10, 2020

About the Author
Frederick Pabst Wurlitzer

The author, Frederick Pabst Wurlitzer, M.D., F.A.C.S. was born in San Francisco, although his four siblings were born in Cincinnati where the family business, The Wurlitzer Music Company, had been located. He was raised drinking Pabst beer while listening to Wurlitzer jukebox music.

Trained at Stanford, the University of Cincinnati, and UCLA, he did a later fellowship in surgical oncology at the University of Texas MD Anderson Hospital in Texas. For a brief stint, he was an Instructor in Surgery at U.S.C. Medical School in Los Angeles. Later, he practiced as an oncological surgeon, and he is still in old age a board-certified surgeon.

Although he has never published anything about Rembert Wurlitzer or The Wurlitzer Music Company before, he has written numerous medical articles published in over seven different medical journals, including the prestigious *Annals of Surgery*, *Vascular Surgery*, *Journal of the American Medical Association (JAMA)*, *Journal of Pediatric Surgery, A.M.A. Archives of Surgery, Plastic and Reconstructive Surgery,* and the *Southern Medical Journal*. Not all medical publications are cited.

After retirement from active surgery in 1988, he volunteered numerous times for doing surgery, usually for a period of about two months each time, in Umtata, South Africa as a C-Section specialist, the Congo, St. Lucia, the Cook Islands as a surgeon for a nation, and about six months in Sierra Leone, West Africa, and elsewhere for a total of close to three years volunteering as a surgeon.

Pay was minimal, but psychological rewards great. Because usually there was no specialist care, he did orthopedics, urology, gynecology, and even occasionally thoracic surgery. Often in West Africa, he gave his own anesthesia.

His original intent on becoming a surgeon had been to work in Africa like Albert Schweitzer, a childhood hero. His short stint tours as a surgeon throughout the world reflected his affection for Albert Schweitzer and love for the poor.

Realizing that he had never worked in the U.S. for the indigent, he obtained a commission as a Commander (O-5) to work briefly in a Public Health hospital serving American Indian nations.

Politically, like most Canadians he is socially a progressive and financially a conservative. He votes as an Independent in the U.S.

He now lives most of the time in Victoria, BC, Canada with his Canadian wife, Ann, who was born in Quebec. They have known each other well for over 55 years.

He can be reached at franwurlit2@gmail.com.

Professional and other Publications (only a few of numerous medical publications are cited):

1. Wurlitzer FP, Ballantyne AJ: Reconstruction of the lower jaw area with a bipedicled delto-pectoral flap and a ticonium prosthesis. Plastic and Reconstructive Surg 1972;49:220-223
2. Wurlitzer FP, Wilson E.: Aorto-Pulmonary anastomoses using autologous pericardium. Vasc Surg 1972;6:128-132
3. Wurlitzer FP, Ayala A, Romsdahl: Extraosseous osteogenic sarcoma. Arch Surg 1972;105:691-695
4. Wurlitzer FP, Ayala A, McBride C.: The problems of diagnosing and treating infiltrating lipomas. Amer Surg 1972;39:240-243
5. Wurlitzer FP, Mares AJ, Isaacs H et al: Smooth muscle tumors of the stomach in childhood and adolescence. J Ped Surg 1973;8:421-427

6. Wurlitzer FP: Improved technique for radical transthoracic forequarter amputation. Annals Surg 1972;177:467-471
7. Wurlitzer FP: Volunteering in West Africa. West J Med 1991;154:730-732

Books by Fred Pabst Wurlitzer

Philosophical Poetry
The Gospel of Fred – 2019
The Second Gospel of Fred - 2019
Love to the Trinity – 2020

Non-Fiction
Rembert – 2020
(Includes the play, *Rembert*)

Children's Books
Spiritual Fairy Tales – 2020
The Seven Deadly Sins – 2020
The Seven Heavenly Virtues – 2020

Stories from the Old Testament
Comic Books with Doggerel
Book 1 Genesis - Part 1 – 2020
Book 2 Genesis - Part 2 – 2020
Book 3 Exodus - Part 2 – 2020
Book 4 Exodus - Part 2 – 2020
Book 5 Number and Deuteronomy– 2020
Book 6 Joshua – 2020
Book 7 Ruth – 2020
Albrecht Dürer's "Kleine Passion" – 2020
Albrecht Dürer's "Grosse Passion" – 2020
Han Holbein's "Dance of Death" – 2020
Albrecht Dürer's "The Crucifixion" – 2020

Made in the USA
Columbia, SC
22 March 2021